Someone to KISS

Someone Series Book 3

Someone to KISS

ROBERT LEWIS

4 Horsemen
Publications, Inc.

Dedication

As **ALWAYS, THIS** is dedicated to my parents—
Robert O. Lewis and Dolores C. Lewis—and to
the diva dog, Bonita.

Table of Contents

1

CIRCUIT PARTY

CAMERON MOVED HIS body to the beat of the house music thumping through the speakers. The shirt he had tucked into the back pocket of his jeans was lost a long time ago. A sheen of sweat coated his smooth bare chest. Surrounded by hot sexy men in similar states, he let himself forget he—very publically—broke up with his fiancé two weeks ago.

For a little while, he was just Cameron: not Alex's ex fiancé, not Sexy Lexi's nephew, not the hottest gossip item of the moment. He could forget that scene at the party he was forced to relive over and over again because the video of it went viral.

Then, there were the memes. They were the worst. They were everywhere.

He didn't have to worry about any of that tonight. Tonight, he could lose himself in the mesh of hard, sweaty bodies, in the exploratory hands groping his cock or cupping his ass. Here, he loses himself in the unspoken promise of sex and drugs, ready and available for those looking for it.

Drugs weren't Cameron's thing, but the sex…the sex was definitely his thing. He figured the best way to heal the hole in his heart was by filling his other hole. Right now, he had eyes on the shirtless, tattooed, muscled stud dancing on the box who would hopefully be filling one or both of his holes. The man was only a few feet away, but on the crowded dance floor it may as well be a million miles.

Moving his hips in time with the music, Cameron raised his arms above his head and twirled in the jumble of men. Casually glancing up with predatory eyes, he saw he succeeded in catching the attention of his prey. Lowering one hand, he ran it down his sweat-sheened chest and past his flat, taut stomach to hook into the top of his low-cut jeans.

The move had the desired effect. The man hopped off the box and shouldered his way to Cameron, and as he approached, hands from the faceless crowd casually roamed his body. An interloper wrapped their arms around the tattooed stud's neck. Cameron was pleased to watch the intruder be spun and released in the throngs of writhing bodies.

When the man finally stood before Cameron, he pulled Cameron against his body. Their bodies were flush, crotches grinding in time with the music. He leaned in for a kiss. Cameron deftly deflected it by turning in the man's arms and grinding his ass into the man's crotch. The man read the message loud and clear.

His lips brushed over Cameron's ear as he spoke just loud enough to be heard, "Let's go to the bathroom."

The man didn't wait for the obvious answer. Taking Cameron by the hand, he plowed through the crowd. The dirty looks they got from the displaced people turned into knowing smiles once they saw where Cameron and his escort were going. He shoved his way into the bathroom where men were loitering about.

A bathroom stall door swung open and three men came stumbling out. Before anyone else could claim the prized available stall, the tattooed man pulled in Cameron. Cameron could hear the protesting shouts from the men they pushed ahead of. Cameron didn't care. They'd get theirs, just like he was about to get his.

In the tiny four-by-four stall, Cameron got a good look at his stud: the etched lines around his eyes, the ruddy brown of his overly tanned skin, and the receding hairline of his short yet overly styled hair. Cameron chose to focus on the bulging, gym-toned, decorated muscles and the outline of the fat, juicy cock in the man's tight shorts.

The man leaned into Cameron. He was zeroing in on Cameron's lips. With a slight panic in his voice, Cameron stopped the man with a hand on his chest and said, "I don't kiss."

If the man was offended, it was not reflected in the grin he gave Cameron. "Cool. Too intimate. I get it. You don't mind shoving your cock down my throat, do you?"

The man suddenly dropped down to his knees and started working open Cameron's jeans. Cameron leaned back against the rickety partition wall. The tattooed man worked down Cameron's jeans to reveal the basic black jock strap underneath. His cock was hard and throbbing in the confines of the cotton pouch. The tattooed man pulled the pouch aside, setting Cameron's ten inch cock free.

Cameron looked down to see the man stroking his cock and grinning triumphantly. "Twinks always have the biggest dicks." He doesn't say this to Cameron, but more to himself. Cameron's cock is pressed to his taut stomach. "Nice set of balls too," he said before burying himself in Cameron's groin.

Cameron closed his eyes, enjoying the feel of the man's soft lips and warm tongue on his balls. Throwing one hand back to grab the top of the partition and the other moving to the back of the man's head, Cameron groaned, "Fuck yeah. Eat those fucking balls."

From one ball to the other, the man worked them while stroking a steady stream of precum out of his own cock. Cameron spread his legs a little further, letting the man slip into the tender area between his thighs and groin. Cameron's legs nearly buckled from the feel of his tongue lapping at the sweat and musk.

The tattooed man moaned into Cameron's skin as his hand continued to pump Cameron's cock, milking streams of precum which ran down Cameron's dick and coated his hand. He seemed perfectly content in prolonging this casual circuit party hook up, but Cameron needed this man on his dick. The men outside waiting needed this stall.

Taking his hand off the partition, Cameron nudged the tattooed man's hand off his cock and replaced it with his own. With his other hand he pushed the man back from his crotch. "Suck my fucking dick," Cameron growled in a lustful voice he didn't recognize.

Cameron aimed, then pulled the tattooed man onto his cock. It slipped easily between the tattooed man's lips and into his hungry throat. Cameron could feel the man's tongue working the underside of his shaft as he held him onto his cock.

The tattooed man's nose was pressed into Cameron's hairless crotch, and he waited for the tattooed man to start coughing and sputtering before letting him off. The man only pulled off until he held the tip of Cameron's cock in his mouth. He felt the tattooed man's tongue running over his crown and brushing over his piss slit.

"Oh, fuck yeah. Swallow that cock," Cameron moaned when his cock disappeared once again down the tattooed man's throat. Cameron's right hand found the tiny nub of his left nipple. Running his thumb over it, Cameron closed his eyes and groaned, "Swallow that fucking cock."

The tattooed man moaned around Cameron's cock. He alternated between fast and slow, stroking the head of Cameron's dick with his tongue when he could. Cameron's dick throbbed with the threat of detonation in the man's mouth, but Cameron needed that one extra push to set him off. He needed this tattooed stud slamming into his ass.

Pulling off Cameron's cock, the tattooed stud began stroking Cameron's cock. "You've got a nice cock man. I need it in me." He stood up quickly and turned around. He lowered the back of his tight shorts to reveal his toasted buns and said, "I'm pre-lubed, so just stick it in."

Cameron hesitated a minute before reaching out and running his hand over the toned ass cheeks. He rarely ever topped. Alex never let him top. Now, running his hand over the tight and firm buttocks presented to him by this tattooed stud, the voice in his head told him to go for it.

"Bend over." Cameron put his hand on the tattooed man's back and pushed him into position. With his other hand, he lined his cock up with the man's prepared hole. He pushed in, sliding easily into the man. Cameron could feel the heat of the tattooed man's body surrounding his cock, the pulsing of the man's insides massaging his dick as he sank deeper and deeper into the man.

"You can take some dick," Cameron commented when he realized he was balls-deep in the tattooed man, and he hadn't even flinched.

The tattooed man grinned back over his shoulder at Cameron. "You don't have to be gentle with me. I can take it."

Cameron tested the tattooed man's words by slowly pulling an inch or so out and slamming back in. The man barely let out a grunt. Cameron took a firmer hold on his hips and thrusted furiously into the tattooed man. His slender hips crashed so hard

into the man's muscled ass he was certain he'd have bruises the next day.

Try as he might, Cameron was just on the brink of his climatic surge. He couldn't quite get to that precipice, though he could feel it churning in his balls screaming to get out. Cameron pumped harder and harder, hoping to reach that point where he would just pop, but he just couldn't.

"Breed me man. Breed my ass," the tattooed man called back to Cameron.

Cameron gritted his teeth. He was right there. He just needed something to trigger him, to unleash what felt like a tidal wave from his bouncing balls into this hot, sexy man. He knew he could just pull his cock out and jerk it out all over this hot stud's ass, but that's not what he wanted. That's not what his tattooed stud wanted.

Cameron closed his eyes. "I'm going to fucking breed you. I'm going to pump you so full." Cameron pictured their roles reversed. The hot tattooed stud was pumping into him, pressing him against the partition wall. "Oh, God." Cameron threw his head back. "Fuck!"

Cameron's ass clenched. His balls drew up, his cock exploding deep inside this nameless tattooed stud. He continued thrusting with short needy thrusts as his dick pulsed inside the man. He felt the tremors of his orgasm reverberate through his body.

Cameron let out a shudder before pulling out. "Damn, I needed that."

"Me, too." The tattooed man stood as he pulled his shorts up over his freshly fucked ass.

Cameron grabbed some tissue off the roll and wiped the remnants of his seed off his cock. The tattooed man was on his knees playing with his sock. Awkwardly Cameron asked, "Do you want me to, um, help you out?"

"Naw, I'm good." The tattooed man stood. He winked at Cameron. "I hope to get a couple more loads before the night is over."

Cameron pulled his pants up and tucked away his dick. "Oh, okay. Well, it was fun."

The tattooed man held out a card. "Hey, do you think you could maybe give your aunt my information? I've got a popular OnlyFans account."

"Sure." Cameron took the card with a phony smile.

The man adjusted his cock in his pants. "Great. Look, it was fun, but I've got more loads to sniff out."

"Go. Do your thing man," Cameron said, playing with the card just to have something to do with his hands.

"Catch you later, man. Oink. Oink." The tattooed man gave Cameron another wink, then left the stall.

Cameron had to push his way through four men claiming the open stall. He quickly exited the bathroom, only stopping at the trash to deposit the tattooed stud's card. This always happened since that damn video went viral. They didn't want *him*. They wanted his connections.

COFFEE AND DISAPPOINTMENT

STEPPING INTO THE tiny coffee shop, Carlos's stomach twisted into nervous knots. It was easy to spot his sister Marisol sitting at a table at the far end of the shop with her usual drink, a Caramel Frappuccino, in front of her. Her long, thick, wavy hair cascaded down to her shoulders, framing her pensive face. When she saw him, her face didn't light up.

I shouldn't have come. Carlos could see the distraught etched on her face. *It's been three years, and she still can't smile when she sees me.*

She didn't even stand to hug him when he approached the table, giving him the weakest smile before he sat down. Carlos was tempted to order a coffee before sitting down, but he knew it would just delay the painful conversation for which he was here. Plus, he'd probably be gone before it came.

They sat for a moment in an uneasy silence before Carlos spoke. "How are you, Marisol?"

"I'm good." Marisol looked everywhere but at him. She then quickly asked, "How are you?"

Shaking his head, Carlos chuckled. He could tell she really didn't care. If she did, she would have helped him when their parents kicked him out at seventeen for being gay and had no place to go. She would have tried to find him in the three years since he had been living on the streets.

Carlos folded his arms on the table and deliberately looked her in the eyes. "Cut the shit, Marisol. I haven't heard from you or anyone else in the family since Mom and Dad kicked me out. You went through all the trouble of getting me a message that you needed to talk to me. Now talk."

Marisol played with the straw in her drink. Carlos saw she was obviously uncomfortable, either from what she had to say, or by simply being here with him. It was when he started to get up from the table that she finally said, "Wait!"

Carlos sat back down. He was beginning to question his judgment in coming here. "Why are you here, Marisol? Why am I here?"

Marisol finally looked at Carlos and said, "We saw the news."

For a moment, Carlos let himself believe they cared. "You guys were worried?"

"No. Well, yes," she blurted, then took a long sip from her Frappuccino to shut herself up.

Disappointed, Carlos asked, "What is it then?"

Marisol stared at her cup. "Everyone knows you do those ... those movies now."

"I do porn," Carlos sighed. "I do gay porn."

Marisol looked around quickly to see if anyone heard him. "Yes," she said in a hushed whisper. "Mom and Dad are so embarrassed. You need to stop."

Carlos didn't even realize he was laughing as he spoke. "Seriously? They are embarrassed by me doing gay porn, but not embarrassed they threw their son out on the streets for being gay?"

"It's not funny. We're a good Christian family. It's shameful for you to be doing this," Marisol whispered angrily.

"Oh, it's *hilarious*," Carlos countered. "Were Mom and Dad being 'good Christians' when they tossed me out onto the streets? Were you being a 'good Christian' when I came to you for help, and you slammed the door in my face?"

"That's not fair!" Marisol shot back louder than she intended. Her eyes darted around to see if her raised voice had caught anyone's attention before settling back on Carlos. "You know we couldn't have your perversions in our homes. I have little children."

Carlos scoffed, his lips curling into an unhappy smile. "So, I'm no longer part of the family but you all can dictate my life?"

"If you had only gone to counseling. You can still go. They can help you with your sickness." Marisol's eyes were big, round and pleading.

Carlos couldn't believe she could be this naive, this blind. "Counseling? I'm not sick, Marisol! I'm gay!"

"Keep your voice down. You're making a scene," Marisol said sternly, seeing the few customers and staff looking at them.

Carlos stood, causing the chair to scrape loudly on the floor. He raised his voice so everyone in the coffee shop could hear him. "My biological family may have turned their back on me, but my new family loves me for who I am. Please, don't contact me again unless you're ready to love me for who I am. Good bye, Marisol."

Carlos stormed out, not noticing the phones out recording his and Marisol's exchange. He hated leaving her there with everyone looking at her with judgmental eyes.

HE'S HERE

EVERYTHING WAS READY. Nathan carefully removed the roast from the oven, and setting it on the counter, he checked the time. His Daddy Lin would be home soon. He removed his apron, the only thing he wore aside from the ball stretcher, and carefully folded it before putting it away. Nathan didn't like wearing any type of clothing. He only put them on only when it was necessary.

The chain leash that was attached to his ball stretcher dragged across the floor as he moved. The thick chain was secured tightly to the center of the living room floor and was just long enough to allow Nathan to do the majority of his duties: cooking, cleaning, preparing for his Daddy Lin. And it was just shy of allowing Nathan to reach the front door or any of the windows.

It didn't matter, though. It was all for show. The tiny cameras all over the house and play room recorded his every move which would be edited and spliced together for the fan sites Daddy Lin managed. Since the house Nathan shared with his Daddy Lin was set far back in a secluded part of the woods, they didn't have to worry about nosey neighbors seeing what they were doing.

They also didn't have any cell or internet service. Daddy Lin would take the finished videos and drive out to the main road to upload them. Sometimes Nathan would go with him, snuggling up against Daddy Lin while he worked in his truck on the side of the road. They hadn't intended to be lovers, but Nathan had fallen for the gentle sweetness of Daddy Lin.

Nathan's heart skipped a beat when the chime rang, alerting him someone was coming up the dirt road drive. *Daddy Lin is coming!* Nathan rushed to put three perfect cubes into a rocks glass before pouring the right amount of Crown Royal whiskey. He eyed the glass, making sure not a drop more or less was in the glass.

Perfect. Nathan smiled, carefully picking up the glass and carrying it into the living room. He dropped to his knees at the designated spot. Bowing his head, he raised the glass with both hands and waited for his Daddy Lin. Today was Friday, and no doubt Daddy Lin and he would be taking full advantage of the Playroom over the weekend. They had videos to make.

Nathan forced himself to keep his eyes on the floor with the sound of the locks clicking open, the door opening smoothly. Nathan heard the familiar sounds of his Daddy Lin's boots on the tile entryway. Fighting the urge to look up, Nathan kept his eyes down and focused on a spot on the floor. This was a game they played—which Nathan loved—for the fans.

Nathan took in a deep breath when he heard the door close and the locks snap. It seemed like forever before the booted feet of Daddy Lin appeared in his line of view. Nathan lowered his arms when the glass was taken from his hands, then went to work removing Daddy Lin's boots.

Nathan held the boot so Daddy Lin could remove one foot, then did the same for the other. Nathan then worked his socks down and off. "Good boy," Daddy Lin said, patting him on the head, and Nathan felt a surge of pride. "Put those away and meet me at my chair."

"Yes, sir." Nathan waited for Daddy Lin to walk past him before standing and taking the shoes. He put the shoes on the rack, and the socks went into the hamper in the adjoining laundry room. Moving to Daddy Lin's side, he kept his head bowed. He stood with his legs apart and his arms behind his back, maintaining the submissive routine for the viewers.

Nathan listened to the clicking of the ice from Daddy Lin swirling his drink. "Did you get all of your chores done?"

Staying in character, Nathan kept his voice soft and quiet, "Yes, sir."

"Good. Now, for me to properly enjoy my cocktail." Daddy Lin's hand wrapped around Nathan's soft cock. Nathan watched Daddy Lin bring the glass up to dip his dick into the cold brown liquid. Nathan held in the gasp while Daddy Lin swirled his cock around the glass. "Just the way I like it."

Daddy Lin pulled Nathan's cock from the glass, and leaning in, took Nathan's cock into his mouth. Nathan shuddered at the sudden warmth and tongue flicking around his cock. Daddy Lin ran his tongue over the head before pulling off Nathan's thickening cock. He repeated the process of dipping Nathan's cock in the glass and sucking the liquor off it over and over again.

Daddy Lin downed the last swallow of Crown before setting the glass on the coffee table. "Cocktails with extra cock. The drink of kings." He put his hand on Nathan's hip to guide him to stand in front of him. "My beautiful boy."

Nathan's pale cheeks flushed red at the compliment. He didn't see himself as beautiful: he had a slender and toned, hairless, five-foot-eight body; tiny ruby-red nipples; and short, stringy brown hair on his head. It was Daddy Lin who told him he was beautiful, and Daddy Lin never lied to him.

It was Daddy who Nathan saw as beautiful with his thick corded muscles, his coppery brown skin from working outdoors, and his clean-shaven bald head. Daddy Lin had rough calloused hands that sent shivers down Nathan's spine when touched. Daddy Lin's squat muscle body was only five-foot-five, but to Nathan he was enormous.

"Let's take this off for a bit," Daddy Lin said, pulling the magnetic ball stretcher apart. He pulled Nathan into his lap. "You'll wear your collar this weekend. I have a guest coming to pay us a visit."

Nathan shifted uneasily on Daddy Lin's lap. He didn't like meeting people. Strangers made him

uneasy. The idea alone was enough to make Nathan panic. "Shh. He's not staying here." Daddy Lin rubbed Nathan's back. "It's okay. If it gets to be too much for you, we can do Private Time. You like Private Time with your Daddy Lin, right?" Nathan smiled shyly. "Daddy Lin likes Private Time with his boy."

Daddy Lin ran the scruff of his beard along Nathan's chest. "Do you know what Daddy Lin really likes?"

"Yes, sir," and Nathan's voice quivered when he spoke.

"Say it." Daddy Lin took one of Nathan's nipples between his teeth.

Nathan gasped from Daddy Lin gently chewing his nipple. Panting, he managed to squeak out, "Daddy Lin likes hearing his boy. He likes to hear his boy enjoying himself."

"That he does," Daddy Lin said, moving his mouth to Nathan's. Kissing Nathan, he began fondling Nathan's cock, running his rough hand up and down Nathan's fully erect, ten-inches and rubbing his thumb over the crown to coat it with Nathan's precum.

Nathan slipped his tongue around Daddy Lin's. His lips felt the scrape of Daddy Lin's whiskers when he deepened the kiss. These tender moments were the ones that eased the panic in Nathan. He needed the soft with the hard, the structure with the carefree. Daddy Lin knew how to balance it for him.

"I think I'll have dessert first," Daddy Lin growled into the kiss. Nathan wrapped his arms around Daddy Lin's neck when he suddenly found himself lifted up. Carefully Daddy Lin stepped around the coffee table and gingerly sat Nathan down on the fluffy couch.

"Do you know how hard it is not to ravage you every single time I see you?"

Nathan smiled shyly, then panicked. "Your food will get cold, sir."

Daddy Lin spread Nathan's legs and knelt between them. "It always tastes better when I have the taste of you in my mouth first." Daddy Lin began running his hands over Nathan's body. "Besides, if it's cold, then I can punish you for it," he teased.

"Please," Nathan begged.

Daddy Lin let out an amused chuckle. "Remember, Daddy Lin will always take care of you and give you what you need." Daddy Lin stroked Nathan's cock. "Right now, Daddy Lin needs this."

This was all still new to Nathan, though. He and Daddy Lin had been together for a year. Nathan's previous Daddy passed away a little over a year ago. Daddy Lin was supposed to help out with the camp next door, after his Daddy passed. Daddy Lin simply took up the mantle of caring for Nathan. Neither had intended this romantic aspect in their relationship. Well, Daddy Lin hadn't, but Nathan couldn't take his eyes off him. It was rocky at first, but Nathan grew comfortable with Daddy Lin. Then, grew bold. Daddy Lin didn't have a chance.

Nathan learned that his Daddy Lin liked to play with his cock. He liked it when Nathan touched him. He liked it when Nathan made sounds and told him what he wanted. He liked it when Nathan snuggled up against him, and Daddy Lin loved to kiss. Some nights they would spend hours just kissing.

Nathan groaned at Daddy Lin's lips surrounding the head of his cock. He ran a tentative hand over Daddy Lin's head, urging him with a slight push to go down further. Daddy Lin continued to play with the tip before slowly working another inch or so down. Nathan whimpered with need. He grew bolder and gave another slight push. Daddy Lin took another inch then backed off. Nathan pushed slightly. Daddy Lin went back down.

Nathan knew what he was doing. Daddy Lin was testing him, to see if he remembered his new rules. He took a deep breath and found his voice. Running his hand over Daddy Lin's smooth scalp, Nathan bit his lip then let out a growly, "Suck me." Nathan was rewarded with Daddy Lin taking more of his cock.

Nathan felt *it*. He couldn't explain it, other than it was like when Daddy Lin unlocked the door. Things just *clicked* in him, and this "door" opened for another Nathan to come out. "Oh, yeah, suck my big dick." Daddy Lin nearly had all of Nathan down his throat. "Take it. Milk my balls dry."

Daddy Lin's hand moved down to cup Nathan's balls. Nathan looked down at Daddy Lin as he began playing with his own tiny nipples. His noises and sounds of pleasure mixed with Daddy Lin's slurps around his iron-hard cock. Daddy Lin knew how to toy with him, to prolong or end any sexual encounter.

"Oh, God yes." Nathan arched his hips up into Daddy Lin's mouth. "Fuck, yeah."

By the feel of Daddy Lin's tongue running along his shaft and toying with his tip, Nathan knew what Daddy Lin wanted to hear him say, but he wanted to

enjoy Daddy Lin's mouth on his cock. Nathan was torn between pleasure and obligation. He couldn't decide, so he did the only thing he could: he let Daddy Lin decide.

Nathan began thrusting his hips up into Daddy Lin's mouth. "That feels so fucking good. You're going to make me blow my load right down your throat."

Daddy Lin took Nathan's balls in one hand, the other he slipped under him. Slipping a finger between his cheeks, Daddy Lin rubbed Nathan's rosebud with his finger. Nathan gasped. This was a tease, a promise for later. Nathan was flooded with the image of Daddy Lin buried between his tiny pert cheeks, lapping the delicate flower.

"I'm going to–" Nathan managed to get out before taking Daddy Lin's head in both hands and thrusting frantically up into Daddy Lin's mouth. Daddy Lin coughed and sputtered around his cock, but did not fight him to get off it. "Ugh!"

Nathan's entire body tensed with the explosion into Daddy Lin's mouth. What felt like a monsoon of cum shot from his balls. Daddy Lin gluttonously swallowed every last bit, remaining there, suckling on the tip of Nathan's cock until the last drops were swallowed. Daddy Lin never let anything go to waste.

"Fuck, I needed that," Nathan sighed, his hands falling to the side and slumping into the couch.

Daddy Lin pulled off his cock then moved up to kiss Nathan. "So did I."

Nathan fell back into character, remembering what the subscribers liked. "Daddy Lin, your dinner."

"You'll warm it up and serve it to me." Daddy Lin pecked Nathan's lips. "Then, I'll give your bottom a good spanking before I pound it."

"Yes, sir." Nathan smiled.

The chime of someone coming up the road sounded. "My friend must be early." Daddy Lin pecked him on the lips again. "Go set the table for four. I'll go outside to greet him." Nathan shifted uneasily under Daddy Lin. "You can wait in the bedroom until I come get you. We'll do this slowly for you."

"Thank you, Daddy Lin." Nathan hugged him.

Daddy Lin peeled himself off Nathan. He winked at Nathan. "You really are a beautiful boy. I'm lucky to have you."

Nathan looked down shyly. "Thank you, Daddy."

"You're welcome. Now get to work." Daddy Lin straightened his polo shirt and headed to the door.

Nathan took a moment to admire the firm ass of his Daddy Lin before getting off the couch and heading into the kitchen. He carefully made four plates of the roast and vegetables he cooked. They were still warm, but Nathan heated the plates anyway. He heard the door open and the taps of booted feet on the tile.

"Daddy Lin?" Nathan called out. When no answer came, he peered around the corner. The door was open, but Daddy Lin was nowhere to be seen. Nathan cautiously moved toward the door. "Daddy Lin?"

Nathan felt the fear building in him with every step toward the door. He didn't remember Daddy Lin putting his boots back on. What if this was one of Daddy Lin's friends? Daddy Lin and he were

working on meeting people, but he wasn't ready to meet someone without Daddy Lin. Nathan swallowed hard as he reached the door. He didn't like to go outside without Daddy Lin.

Heart racing, Nathan looked outside. Daddy Lin was sprawled out on the ground and Nathan screamed, "Daddy Lin!" A hood came down over Nathan's head. He shrieked. Two strong arms came around Nathan and dragged him back into the house. He kicked and flailed, trying to free himself so he could get to Daddy Lin.

"Fucking freak," snarled a deep voice Nathan didn't recognize. "Calm down or I'll go out there and put a bullet in his head." Nathan went limp, praying his Daddy Lin was alright and would come rescue him. "That's better. Be a good boy and no one will get hurt."

GET YOUR SHIT TOGETHER

I**T WAS NEARLY** noon when the car dropped Cameron off at the front door of his Aunt Lexi's place. He was planning on just slipping in and heading up the stairs to the room he'd been sleeping in without Aunt Lexi hearing him. Of course, she was waiting for him in the foyer. He gave her a sheepish smile, knowing there was no escaping her.

He had been expecting this for a while now. She said nothing, giving him that look which told him they were going to have one of their heart-to-hearts. The silence between them spoke volumes. She motioned with her perfectly manicured finger for Cameron to follow her.

For a moment, he debated turning around and running. It wouldn't stop his Aunt Lexi; she would hunt him down. It wouldn't be hard. The only other place he had to go was his condo which he had shared with his cheating bastard ex-fiancé. He couldn't go there because the bastard still hadn't moved out.

The only real choice, the adult choice, was to follow her out onto the patio. She sat down at the lone table and waited for Cameron to join her. He knew everything she was about to tell him came from a place of love. She had raised him since he was thirteen after he lost his mother. Had it not been for Lexi, he could have ended up lost in the foster care system.

Cameron felt Lexi's eyes on him, studying him. She pursed her lips in thought. "It's time to get your shit together," she finally said.

"Okay," Cameron said when she didn't continue. She motioned for him to continue. Cameron sighed. "I'll call Alex and tell him to get out."

"You can give him two weeks." Lexi winked at him. "Meanwhile, I got you a job as PA for a film Josh Star is doing. You fly out in a couple of hours. He's filming at some gay campground in the woods."

Cameron scoffed, "Woods? You know I don't do camping."

"It's not camping. There are cabins and indoor plumbing." She pointed a finger at Cameron. "You need to start using that degree I paid for, and you need to unplug for a while. They don't have WIFI or cell service, so you can decide how you're going to get your shit together. Hopefully everyone will have forgotten all about you and that asshole by the time you get back."

Cameron put his head in his hand. "Some hot muscle stud took me into the bathroom last night to fuck. He had the nerve to hand me his card to give to you."

"Trash can?" Lexi groaned.

"Trash can," Cameron huffed. "I did go home with a hot Brazilian couple though."

Lexi perked up with interest. "Oh? Hot? Big dicks?"

"Yes, on the hot *and* on the big dicks," Cameron smiled coyly.

"And?" Lexi pried.

Cameron laughed, "Hottest sex ever."

Lexi stood. Extending her hand out to Cameron, she said, "You can give me the details while I help you pack."

"Do I really have to go? People die in the woods," Cameron groaned, taking her hand.

She pulled him to his feet. "Yes, and you get to travel with all the equipment. Fun!"

MASKED DISTRACTION

CARLOS WAS HAPPY for the distraction of work when he got home. Hunter had been giving him a crash course in editing. After Barry, they decided it best they all wear multiple hats in production. Topher quit after they arrested Barry, and they were skittish about hiring new people.

Carlos sat back in the office chair and watched the work on the large screen. This was something new they were trying. They had an eager, yet reluctant new actor, Mask. They had gone to great efforts to hide his true identity, including editing out the small heart tattoo on his ass and having him wear a domino mask.

The scene opened. Mark was lying naked on his stomach on the huge lounge bed by the pool. His tanned brown skin shined from sunscreen massaged into it. The screen cut to a close-up of his broad shoulders before slowly traveling down the gentle slope of his back, then up his sun-kissed golden butt cheeks.

The picture lingered on his perfectly toned butt giving the viewer a chance to appreciate the firm roundness of it, then moved down Mark's body, down his thick-muscled thighs and past his calves. It was almost criminal such a beautiful sight ended with the camera panning over to the pool edge.

Two hands rose to grip the pool's edge. Lifting his body up, viewers would get their first view of Mask with his short blond hair weighed down by water around his scalp. They would then get to see his soon-to-be-trademarked diamond mask wrapped around his steely blue eyes. Then they would see that rugged handsome face with water dripping down his angular, stern jaw line.

Carlos watched Mask slowly raise himself up out of the water with his bulging biceps. His sculpted broad chest slowly came into view with water cascading down through his chest hair. He got to see how Mask's body narrowed to a perfect V while watching rivulets of water run through the defined channels of his six pack.

The top of Mask's neatly trimmed blonde pubic hair came into view. It stayed there, teasingly, before one thickly muscled leg came up to the ledge and lifted him out of the water, giving the viewer a full view of his magnificent naked body with his seven-inch-thick cock swaying back and forth.

Mask's left hand came up to push his hair back. His bicep flexed. It looked as big and round as a bowling ball. He stood there, body glistening with water. Had it not been for his bronze brown skin, Carlos would have thought he was looking at a Greek statue of a

sex god. Carlos made a mental note to have Mask help him in his workouts.

The angle changed. Now Carlos could see Mask standing at the pool's edge and Mark lying down. Mark pretended to be unaware as Mask moved with slow deliberate intent. The image changed again. Now Carlos was looking over the hill tops of Mark's ass, Mask was on the other side, out of focus.

Mask's body slowly came into focus as he moved to lay beside Mark. The image on the screen still showed Mark's ass, but now it showed Mask's caressing hand running over the glorious globes. The image zoomed out, showing Mask laying on his side, propped up by an elbow beside Mark.

This was Carlos's favorite part. There was a gentle tenderness to the moment. Mark was still pretending to be sleeping while Mask gingerly rubbed his bottom. Mask leaned over and began kissing Mark's shoulder blade. The kisses were soft and sensual. Carlos wonder if he'd ever get to experience such tenderness.

Mark began to stir. He turned his head and gave Mask the sweetest of smiles. Their mouths touched, lightly at first. The kiss deepened. Carlos didn't just see the passion between the two, he could feel it. The way their lips brushed over one another's, the way they touched each other.

There was a familiarity between the two that was being communicated through the screen. Mask started kissing his way down Mark's neck. He shifted his body as he slowly kissed his way down Mark's sun baked back. He reached Mark's ass and planted wet wistful kisses on each cheek.

They moved wordlessly, Mark arching his back up, Mask settling behind him. Mask spread Mark's cheeks, showing the world his hairless hole. Mask's face then entered the picture. His tongue came out and ran slow circles around Mark's rim. Carlos could feel himself get aroused.

The moaning that can be heard is no doubt coming from Mark, and so is the gasp when Mask rapidly flicked his tongue into Mark. Mask's pink tongue went back to the slow circles then randomly darted. This caused Mark to alternate between moans and groans with a slight whimper every so often.

Mask's right hand went under Mark to stroke his hard leaking cock. Mask ran his tongue from the top of his crack to the tip of his cock before returning back to the top. The sounds Mark made were a blend of moans, groans, gasps and whimpers with one sound fading seamlessly into the other.

Mark's hole was shiny with spit. Mask changed position again, this time slipping under Mark, and taking the flared head of his six-inch cock his mouth. Mark moved his legs back, getting into a modified push up position. Mask's hands came around Mark to take a cheek in each hand. He pulled Mark down into his mouth. You could see the corded muscles of Mark's back as he raised and lowered his hips into Mask. Ringed by Mask's lips, Mark's cock slid easily in and out of his mouth.

Mask's hands moved. They now had Mark's cheeks parted and had a finger dipped into his valley stroking the soft skin. Mark rolled off Mask and they moved to lay side by side. Mask's mouth was back on

Mark in an instant. Mark's mouth wrapped around Mask's swollen cock.

They savored each other's cocks, slowly suckling on each other's cock. Mask's hand was back on Mark's ass, toying with his hole. Mark's hips began moving, fucking himself on Mask's finger and thrusting his cock into Mask's mouth. Mark's movements were slow at first, but sped up with his need to be filled.

Unable to deny himself any longer, Mark rolled Mask onto his back. Straddling Mask's narrow waist, Mark lowered himself onto the engorged cock. The sheer bliss and enjoyment was evident on Mark's face from slowly filling himself with Mask's cock.

Resting on Mask's hips, Mark let out a sigh. Mark rocked his hips. Mask's hands came up and explored his body. Mark let out a shudder at the feather-like touch brushing lightly over his chest, his nipples, down his waist, to rest on his hips.

The two moved in orchestrated symphony. Mark controlled the tempo, rising and falling onto Mask. Each impale caused Mark's eyes to glaze over for a moment. He leaned forward, resting his hands on either side of Mask's head. They kissed, a brief yet sensual peck on the lips.

Mask took the moment to regain the lead. Holding Mark's hips, he began pumping his cock up. Mark arched his back, his head going back in slow stretch of his neck. They rolled, Mark was on his back with his legs hooked on Mask's shoulders. Mask ran his cock in and out of Mark furiously.

Mark's hands were on Mask's back, and his fingers dug into Mask's hard flesh. There was a roll of

Mask's hips and then another. The thrusts randomly went from short and fast to slow and deep. Their mouths came together again, a hot and hungry kiss.

They shifted seamlessly again, Mark getting on all fours while Mask got behind him. Mark arched his back with the careful push of Mask's cock into him. With one hand on his shoulder, Mask fucked Mark. Mark met each of Mask's thrusts with the same vigor and enthusiasm.

Mark's arms and legs seemed to give out and Mask was on top of him, humping relentlessly into him. They rolled to their side. Mask lifted one of Mark's legs so he could get a better angle. Mark turned his head and the two were engaged in another passionate kiss while Mark began stroking his cock.

Mark's hand flew over his cock while Mask jack-hammered into him. You could see it in their faces, the impending eruption. You could see it in the faces of both men that they were on the brink of a cataleptic personal explosion. With their hurried movements it became a race to see who would climax first.

When the moment came, it was Mask that crossed the finish line first. He pulled out. Mark rolled onto his back. Mask was on his knees between Mark's legs, feverishly beating his cock. White spunk shot from his dick, blanketing Mark's cock and stomach.

Mark's body began to jerk. A gusher of white cream shot from his cock, mixing with Mask's load on his stomach, reaching up to his chest and nearly hitting his chin. Bolt after bolt shot forth until Mark laid spent on the pool lounge. Mask fell on top of him,

the results of their encounter smearing across their bodies. A final lustful kiss and the scene faded out.

Carlos adjusted himself. Porn wasn't something that turned him on anymore, but this scene … this scene had. It was hot. It was sensual. It was intriguing. He was so enthralled by what he was watching, he almost forgot to take editing notes. One note he wrote was that *he* wanted to make scenes like this.

"So what did you think?" Hunter's voice startled Carlos from his thoughts.

Carlos shifted in his chair. "That was hot. There were a few spots where we missed covering up Mask's tattoo, and I think we should change a few angles."

"Thanks. It always helps to have an extra set of eyes looking over your work. Remember that." Hunter sat down across the desk. "Are you all packed for your trip?"

Carlos shrugged, "Yeah. I think getting away for a while will do me good."

"I'm sorry about your family." Hunter got up and moved around the desk. Kneeling down in front of Carlos, Hunter took his hands and said, "Remember we're your family now, too. No matter what happens, you'll always have a place with us."

Carlos gave Hunter a weak smile, then raised an eyebrow. "What do you mean no matter what happens?"

Hunter sighed. "Dennis doesn't know when he'll be ready to film again, and Mark and I are thinking of getting our own place in the city. You're more than welcome to come with us."

"I need to decide what I want to do." Carlos gave Hunter's hands a squeeze. He was going to be

homeless again, it seemed. "Don't worry about me. I'll survive."

"Hey." Hunter let go of Carlos's hand and cupped his chin. "I'm serious. You're like a son to us. One we fuck on occasion, but we're serious about you coming to stay with us if you want."

"Carlos has two daddies," he laughed. "Thank you." Carlos leaned forward and hugged Hunter. "You guys have been more family to me than my actual family has been."

"Like I said, we'll always be your family." Hunter hugged him back. "Now, you need to get going, and don't be speeding in my truck."

"I won't," Carlos lied. "Walden Woods, here I come."

PLAYROOM

IN THEIR PLAYROOM, fear gripped Nathan. Huddled in the corner of the dog cage, he had screamed in terror as the two men shoved him in and locked the cage. He had curled up into a little ball and did his breathing exercises when they left, only to feel that surge of panic when the men returned followed by three more men.

Nathan drew comfort from the cage. In here, he told himself, he was safe. He couldn't be seen by the strangers if he stayed in his corner and stayed quiet. They wouldn't notice him and he could close his eyes and pretend they weren't there. He took slow deep breaths, using the exercises he learned from his therapist to quiet the growing storm of anxiety that threatened to wash over him.

He quietly watched the three new men forced into the jail cell at gunpoint by the other two. The men spoke angrily at each other, but Nathan couldn't hear them over the raging storm in his head. He watched the jailed men strip down to their underwear and hand their clothes through the bars before the two armed men left with their things.

Nathan wasn't sure how long it was between when the jailed men were brought in and the other two men returned, dragging Daddy Lin's limp naked body. Nathan held in his screech. Daddy Lin had two blackened eyes. His lip was bloodied and bruises decorated his body. He wanted to go tend to Daddy Lin, but the two scary men were there.

Nathan watched the men drop Daddy Lin onto the floor. They bound Daddy Lin's wrists behind his back with leather restraints, then did the same with his feet, sliding a lock into each to prevent anyone from freeing him. They attached Nathan's favorite collar around Daddy Lin's neck, then attached a chain to it that they hooked onto the wall. Last, they fitted Daddy Lin's mouth with a leather gag. The muscular man with black hair spat on Daddy Lin before they left.

Nathan was gathering his courage when the skinny older man with stringy blonde hair came in with food and water. Nathan knew the man from his old Daddy Walden. He had come to visit every so often. Nathan always hid from him. His face was always in a perpetual scowl. He and Old Daddy Walden would often yell at each other before he would leave angry.

Nathan closed his eyes and covered his ears when the man came near his cage. He felt the cage rattle when the man opened the cage door, then again when he shut it. Nathan counted to one hundred before he opened his eyes. The blonde scary man left a sandwich and a bottle of water for him.

Cautiously, Nathan took the food. He looked over and saw the men in the jail were eating the same thing, so he figured it was safe. Carefully he took a small bite, trying to taste if there was anything strange in the sandwich. When he was certain it was safe, he inhaled the sandwich and downed the water.

When Nathan was done, he instantly felt guilty when he saw Daddy Lin going without. He reached out a hand to the cage door to test the lock when the play-room door opened again. The two scary men returned. They moved straight to Daddy Lin, nudging him with their feet. The hulking brunette spat on Daddy Lin again before the two spoke angrily at each other. This time Nathan forced himself to listen.

"You said there would be money here, Corbin," The hulking brunette snapped.

Corbin, the scowling blonde snapped back, "There is, we just have to find it."

The hulking brunette grabbed Corbin by the collar and lifted him up. "There better be. Getting revenge on this piece of shit isn't enough for me to be risking jail for this shit."

"Rafi, calm down." Corbin's feet dangled in the air. "I know there is. Walden told me he kept his treasure here. He said it was here safe and sound where no one would find it. We just have to find it."

Rafi dropped Corbin onto his feet. He pointed at the three men in the jail cell. "And what about them? What are going to do with them? You didn't tell me we were going to have to deal with a porn crew, too. You said it was just these two."

"I didn't know they were coming," Corbin answered, straightening his shirt. "By the time anyone finds them locked up in here, we'll be long gone. No one comes up here. It might be months or years before someone thinks to come check on anyone here."

Rafi walked over to Nathan's cage. Nathan scurried to the far end away from him. "Seems to me your plans have lots of holes in them." Rafi shook the cage, scaring Nathan. There was a cruel smile on his face. "I say we find the money, take them for a little walk in the woods, and do a little target practice."

"We can do that, if you want," Corbin's voice was placating. "We need to find the money first."

Rafi turned to face Corbin, an evil sneer on his face. "Find it. Quickly. Tear that whole fucking house apart if you have to, but find it." He pointed to Daddy Lin. "That little bitch cost me everything when he accused me of rape. No studio will hire me now."

"He was asleep when you went into his room and fucked him." Corbin took a cautious step back. "Or, that's what the news said."

"He didn't say no, now did he?" Rafi shoved Corbin out of his way. "Now help me find that damn money."

Nathan watched Corbin slink out behind Rafi. He prayed they did not come back. What they said stuck in his head. These men were planning on hurting him, Daddy Lin, and the men in the jail. He had to do something to save them. He had to be brave. He had to remember and trust in his therapy.

INTO THE WOODS OR
WASH MY BACK?

CAMERON WAS IN a foul mood when he arrived at Walden Woods. The airline had lost his luggage. They managed to get all the video equipment there safely, but he had to lug it all by himself to the rented SUV. He had to drive an hour to get here, only to find out he'd have to share a luxury cabin with one of the actors because the other cabins were being renovated.

"I'm so sorry," The skinny twink with a country lisp said, batting his eyes at Cameron. "There is one cabin open, but you have to use the communal bathroom, and there isn't any AC."

Cameron had to remind himself he wasn't a guest here—that he was here to work—to keep himself from snapping at the young, barely legal boy. Lexi had gotten him this job, and he was a direct reflection on her. He knew better than to piss her off. Plus, he was trying to build his own brand.

"It's fine," Cameron said, the agitation evident in his voice. "The airline is supposed to send my luggage when they find it. Can you make sure it gets to me?"

"Of course! Do you need anything until it gets here? Clothes? Toothbrush?" The young man's chipper attitude grated on Cameron's nerves. "You look about my size. I can lend you some shorts and shirts until your stuff gets here."

Cameron took in a deep breath and let it out, releasing all the anger before he took it out on this helpful young man. "Thank you. That would be great. Just a couple of things. I'm sure they'll get me my things in a day or so."

"Oh, no problem. I'm Ryan, by the way." Ryan came around the desk and extended his hand. "Let me show you to your cabin. I'm actually surprised that you and that other guy showed up since the director and his crew never did."

Cameron, dumbfounded, took Ryan's hand. "Excuse me?"

"Yeah, they were supposed to come yesterday, but they never showed up," Ryan blabbered on chipperly. "We figured they canceled the filming. Mitch and Dean were really bummed about it. Cody and Brad said they were, but I think they were relieved." Ryan lowered his voice conspiratorially. "Brad and Cody have major crushes on each other and are too chicken shit to do anything about it. Cody gets all tongue tied and flustered anytime Brad just takes his shirt off. Brad finds any excuse to take his shirt off in front of Cody. Oh, my God, can you imagine them together? It would be so hot."

Cameron closed his eyes, trying his best not to explode. He had just traveled across the country, lost his luggage, and now he was finding out the director wasn't even here. "Hold on. What do you mean the director didn't show up?" Ryan cocked his head quizzically at Cameron. "I just flew here with all the equipment to film and you're telling me the director and his staff aren't here?"

"Uh, yeah," Ryan answered with a questioning tone. "Shouldn't you know that since you, like, work for him?"

Cameron let go of his hand and did everything he could to keep from going nuclear. "I just got hired yesterday." He took a moment. He was jet-lagged and having a bad day. He didn't want to take it out on this sweet kid. "Can you just show me to my cabin? I'll deal with all this after a hot shower and maybe a nap."

"Sure," Ryan said cautiously. "Your roomie is a real sweetheart. All the guys love him. I think he's out hiking in the woods with Mitch and Brad." Ryan stopped his rambling when he saw the irritation on Cameron's face. "Let's get you to the cabin. It's just up the way a bit."

Cameron got back in the SUV and let Ryan navigate. He took the time to play tour guide, pointing out all the amenities. "That's the barracks. It's where me and the guys hunker down at." Cameron briefly glanced at the long ranch-style cabin as the SUV bounced onward on the dirt road. "Over there is the Fort. That's where you go if you want a little extra kink in your naughty."

Cameron didn't respond, but looked at the small warehouse-looking building. "Out there is where people can pitch their tents, if you know what I mean." Cameron looked to his left to see a sign that said *Hiking Trails.* "We're coming up on the cabins now."

Cameron was a little surprised when they arrived in a clearing. About twenty or so cabins were arranged in a U shape around a beautiful swimming pool. "Behind those is the latrine for all the bathroom needs. You're lucky. Your cabin has its own," Ryan explained. "There's also a communal cantina guests can use. Oh, make a right."

Cameron steered the SUV away from the cabins and pool calling his name. "You're staying in Lake Side," Ryan said it as if it were an honorific. "It's a one bedroom, but has its own bathroom and, more importantly, air conditioning. It's also close to the dock, but don't go jumping in the lake."

"Alligators?" Cameron asked, slowing the SUV to a stop in front of the cabin.

Cameron let out a little laugh. "Not that I've seen. The lake is polluted from before we took over. We're planning on cleaning it up, but anyone who goes in it gets really sick. Of course, why would you want to with that beautiful pool, right?"

Cameron turned off the SUV. Realizing Ryan would need a ride back to the office, he asked, "Hey, do you need a lift back to the office?"

Ryan unbuckled his seat belt and hopped out. "Oh, no. I'll just grab one of the four-wheelers from the cabin area. Do you need help getting that equipment into the cabin?"

Getting out, Cameron looked at the back of the SUV with disdain. "If we don't have a director or staff, I'm guessing we won't be filming."

"That's a bummer." Ryan kicked the ground. "We were looking forward to being in our first official porn."

It finally clicked for Cameron. "Wait, you guys were the talent for the movie?"

"Yeah. Oh, and here." Ryan came around to hand Cameron a key. "I'll come back in a bit with some clothes. If you don't answer, I'll leave them by the door for you."

Cameron really wanted to hate Ryan, but couldn't. "Thank you. You are too sweet."

"Think nothing of it." Ryan winked at him. "You know, just throwing this out there. We have the equipment to film and the talent. If you want to, maybe film something, I'm sure I can talk the boys into it."

Cameron was almost tempted. He wasn't sure if it was the exhaustion or his own ambition that had him considering it. "I'm not really a director. Not yet."

"I'm not really a porn actor, but I was willing to give it a try. Be back in a bit." Cameron watched Ryan trot up the road.

He let himself into the cabin and was surprised at how nice it was compared to its rustic outward appearance. The place looked more like a luxury hotel room instead of a cabin. It had mock hardwood floors, baby blue walls, and white curtains that let in just the right amount of light.

Cameron explored further. The main living area had a gray fluffy couch flanked by its two fluffy armchair companions. In the wall in front of the couch

stood a stone fireplace which cried out for a fire. Between the fireplace and couch was a glass coffee table with a beautiful assortment of wildflowers in a vase.

The bedroom was just as nice as the living area: an enormous queen size bed set in the middle with night stands on either side, an oak chest at the base and matching dresser along the wall. The bathroom was just off the bedroom and it boasted dual sinks in a granite countertop and a walk-in shower that could house at least four people.

Cameron didn't even think about it when he started pulling off his clothes and began running the shower. He just needed to wash the stench of travels off him. Leaving his clothes in a pile on the floor, he stepped in and let the water rain down over him. He saw soap and shampoo, probably from his roomie.

Cameron decided whoever he was sharing the cabin with wouldn't mind. They'd appreciate he was clean. He started soaping his body; it felt so good to wash. He was tired before, but this cleansing seemed to bring new life into him. He was shampooing his hair when the voice of a stranger scared him.

"Ryan left you some clothes," Cameron wiped a clear spot on the steamed-up shower glass. "Mind if I join you? I got a bit muddy on that hike."

"Uh, um. Sure," Cameron said, taking in the gorgeous Latino twink with his smooth almond brown skin. "Be my guest."

"Thanks." Carlos sat Cameron's clothes on the counter, then quickly stripped out of his own muddy clothes. Cameron tried not to stare at the large

swinging meat between his legs. Stepping into the shower, he got under the spray. Their bodies were so close in the large shower.

Stepping back from the spray and away from Cameron, he extended a hand out. "I almost forgot. I'm Carlos. Carlos Ramirez. I really need to start remembering to introduce myself before I get naked."

Cameron took the hand. "Cameron. Cameron Mitchell."

"Nice to meet you, Cameron Mitchell." Carlos pulled Cameron into him, catching him when their bodies collided. "Wash my back?"

THE LATIN LOVE AND
THE CHIPMUNK

CARLOS QUIETLY GAVE the young man in the shower a once-over before announcing himself. He hadn't planned on being naked under the raining water with their bodies pressed against one another, yet here he was. From the press of Cameron's excitement into his thigh, he didn't mind.

Their mouths were so close to touching. If Carlos turned his head just slightly and leaned in, they'd be lost in a kiss. With his hand firmly on the small of Cameron's back, Carlos was tempted to dip it down and get a firm handful of what looked to be a firm plump ass.

"I'm done actually. In the shower that is." It wasn't lost on Carlos that Cameron hadn't tried to pull away when he said the words.

Carlos gazed into his brown eyes. He couldn't explain it. Something about this guy fascinated him. "Wash my back first?"

When he leaned in for a kiss, Cameron turned his head quickly. "I don't kiss."

"That's okay. I do." Carlos didn't want to let go of him, but let his hand slide away when Cameron pulled away. He grabbed the soap and washcloth and handed them to Cameron before turning around. "Get it nice and soapy back there. I want to be squeaky clean for the shoot."

He felt Cameron's tentative cloth-covered hand running circles over his back. "Didn't you hear? The director and his crew didn't show. There isn't going to be a shoot."

Carlos turned around when it was obvious Cameron wasn't going to go any lower than the small of his back. "Why not? You brought the equipment. We have the talent. I can give everyone a crash course in filming."

"Because we can't," Cameron blurted out, beginning to feel a bit flustered. "I need to dry off and take a nap." He handed the washcloth back to Carlos.

Carlos caught him by the waist before he could escape. "You're tense. Why don't you dry off and go wait for me on the bed. Let me relieve you of some of that tension."

"Are you trying to seduce me?" Carlos heard the catch in his voice.

Carlos licked his lips. "Maybe."

"Oh, you're suave. You play the Latin lover part well," Cameron all but laughed.

Carlos stared intently into Cameron's eyes. "I don't play the Latin lover part, I *am* the Latin lover. I could be *your* Latin lover." Carlos gave a wicked smile. "Go wait for me on the bed, and I'll kiss away that stress when I get out."

"I told you I don't kiss." Cameron slipped away and out of the shower.

Carlos took a moment to appreciate Cameron's ass. "I told you that's okay because I do."

Carlos smiled at that dismissive noise Cameron made while he dried off. He took his time soaping up his body, giving Cameron the chance to dry off and decide what he wanted to do. He wasn't normally this aggressive with guys, but Cameron was beautiful. When he looked into Cameron's eyes, he almost melted.

Turning off the water and stepping out of the shower, Carlos noted the clothes he brought in from Ryan were still on the vanity. He took his time drying off, building the anticipation. He could tell Cameron wasn't just a fuck. He was something to be savored and treasured. If he didn't have a shoot to do, he would be buried balls-deep in Cameron all night long.

Stepping into the bedroom, Carlos found Cameron in the middle of the bed, splayed out on his back, arms and legs akimbo. He took a moment to admire Cameron. His slender body, the hint of abdominal muscles on his flat stomach and the huge cock that reached up past his belly button leaking precum.

Fuck. Carlos moved onto the bed, careful not to disturb the beautiful man.

Cameron pretended to ignore his presence, even when Carlos covered his body with his own. He brushed Cameron's wet hair off his forehead. He leaned in for a kiss. Cameron's eyes shot open in terror. He planted a soft kiss on Cameron's forehead.

"Just because you don't kiss, doesn't mean I can't kiss you," and Carlos smiled impishly down at Cameron. "Now, just lay there and relax my little Chipmunk. Let this Latin lover do his thing."

Carlos felt Cameron relax under him before he said, "Okay."

"Now close your eyes, Chipmunk. I got you." Carlos stroked Cameron's cheek with the back of his hand. He saw the slight hesitation in Cameron's eyes before he closed them.

Carlos moved the hand from Cameron's cheek to run a finger over his luscious forbidden lips. He felt Cameron stiffen with a sharp intake of breath, but then he relaxed, blowing out all his stress when he exhaled. Carlos was tempted to steal a kiss, but decided he wanted Cameron to give it to him.

Carlos started with a feather-light kiss on Cameron's left cheek, then to his right and down to his chin. His mouth found the soft crook of Cameron's neck. He sucked gently, running his tongue in slow random patterns over Cameron's silky skin. He took his time, moving along Cameron's neck before slowly moving further down.

Carlos travelled down to Cameron's left nipple, leaving a path of kisses in his wake. He surrounded Cameron's strawberry-red nipple with his lips. His tongue ran leisurely over the nub causing Cameron's

breath to catch. With just the lightest of touches, Carlos ran his teeth over the tiny nub.

Moving from one nipple to the other, Carlos drew lazy loops with his tongue. He could feel Cameron tense with the anticipation. Carlos surrounded the tiny nub with his mouth and lathered it with his tongue. Pulling away slightly, he blew a gentle stream of air on it.

The nub raised and hardened. The area around his nipple pebbled. Carlos danced his fingertips along Cameron's sides. Cameron let out a restrained moan. Carlos latched onto the nipple, his tongue whipping around the skin. With a gasp, Cameron arched his hips up into Carlos.

Letting go of the nipple, Carlos reached up and stroked his hair. "I got you, Chipmunk," Carlos said softly before resuming his expedition down Cameron's body.

Carlos bathed Cameron's flat stomach with kisses. He spelled his name with his tongue across Cameron's stomach, marking him with an invisible sex tattoo. Cameron's stomach fluttered with the touch, and his fingers came to run through his thick, wavy, black hair. Carlos continued his trek downward.

A groan of impatience came from Cameron when Carlos's cheek nudged his hard cock aside. Carlos kissed a path down Cameron's groin. He went down past the throbbing length of Cameron's cock. He spread Cameron's legs. Taking Cameron's cock and aiming it to the sky, he began stroking the mighty missile.

Carlos ran his tongue in lazy circles over Cameron's balls. He took one then the other in his mouth, fondling each in his mouth delicately, moving seamlessly from one to the other. Rolling the smooth precious orbs in his mouth, Carlos realized he almost forgot what it was to have unscripted sex.

Carlos ventured upward with his tongue, licking up the underside of Cameron's shaft, swirling his tongue around the crown, and then slowly running his tongue back down. He heard the hitch of expectancy and the sigh of disappointment in Cameron's breath when Carlos did not wrap his lips around him.

Carlos did this over and over, building the hope that this time he might take Cameron into his mouth. It wasn't until Cameron's whimpers grew so filled with need that Carlos finally decided to stop denying himself as well. He swirled his tongue over Cameron's crown, precum coating his tongue.

With a kiss on Cameron's tip, Carlos let Cameron's cock slide between his lips. Cameron's body vibrated with the groan of satisfaction. Carlos would not be rushed, though. He took his time, slowly working Cameron down while running his tongue over the fleshy hard rod. Carlos liked this, letting go and enjoying himself.

With his hands fisting Carlos's hair, Cameron groaned out, "Fuck, you're driving me crazy."

Carlos slowly pulled up from the base of Cameron's dick to the tip. Twirling his tongue over Cameron's head, he inched his way down again. With Cameron's steely hard cock down his throat, Carlos

rutted in his groin. This time when he made his path back up, he did it at a snail's pace.

"I swear to God, if you don't quit playing I'm going to kick you out of this cabin!" Cameron howled at the top of his lungs.

Holding Cameron's cock with one hand, Carlos pulled off him with a wet pop of his lips. Grinning up at the exasperated Cameron, Carlos said, "This is my cabin, Chipmunk."

"Shut up and suck me." Cameron put a hand on the back of Carlos's head and pulled him back down. When Carlos began toying with the tip again, Cameron threatened, "There are plenty of places in the woods to hide a body."

The comment almost caused Carlos to choke on the dick in his mouth. He decided to give into Cameron's wishes, though at first he moved down slowly. He sped up his slide along Cameron's length. Cameron's cock throbbed in his mouth. He was tempted to slow down and drag out the tease, but by the way Cameron was fisting his hair, Carlos knew Cameron wouldn't allow it.

"Don't stop. Yes. Fuck. Yeah." Cameron's breathe quickened. Carlos knew he had teased the boy too much. "I'm going to—"

Cameron's cock exploded in Carlos's mouth. Carlos continued sucking until Cameron's balls dribbled the last of their juices into his mouth and Cameron's cock softened. Letting Cameron's cock slip from his mouth, Carlos kissed the softening flesh. He moved up Cameron's body so he could look into his eyes.

"That was awesome," Cameron purred, stretching his body under Carlos. "Okay, your turn."

Carlos kissed the top of his head. "I'll collect after we shoot the scenes."

"We're not filming without a director or crew," Cameron sighed sleepily.

Carlos ground his hard cock into Cameron. "Well, Chipmunk, you're not getting this dick until after we film." Carlos kissed his forehead again. "Take a nap. I'll wake you for dinner."

Carlos reluctantly got off Cameron and the bed. He could feel Cameron's eyes on him while he pulled a pair of shorts out and slipped into them. Tucking his hard dick into his shorts, he turned around and gave Cameron a wink. Cameron rolled his eyes with a smile. Carlos liked that smile and the satisfied look on Cameron's face.

"Get some sleep. We've got a porn to shoot." Carlos couldn't take his eyes off the sexy man in his bed.

"We're not filming," Cameron argued.

"Guess you're not getting any of this Latin lover dick." Carlos smiled devilishly. He saw Cameron's cock returning to life. Reaching over and tapping on the hardening member. "I'll tell the boys the shoot is still on."

Carlos turned and walked out of the bedroom. He heard Cameron yell from behind him, "We're not filming!"

"We'll see!" he yelled back, shutting the cabin door behind him.

STORIES IN THE PLAYROOM

NATHAN SHIVERED IN his cage. He had slept off and on since the mean men put him in the cage. Every time he woke in a panic, quickly looking to his bound Daddy Lin for signs of life. The panic would slowly ebb when he saw the slight movement of Daddy Lin's breathing and the guilt would seep in for not being able to help him.

The men in the jail tried to talk to him, but eventually gave up when Nathan ignored them. He still hadn't built the courage to talk to them. He knew they had to be friends of Daddy Lin, but he didn't know them. They could be as nice as Daddy Lin or as cruel as the two men. Right now he was safe from their hands, but cruel words were not stopped by bars.

Nathan's heart leapt when he saw Daddy Lin's eyes creep open. He groaned in pain through the gag. Nathan watched with eager anticipation as Daddy Lin slowly regained consciousness, sleepily struggled to move, and then alarm exploding on his face when he realized his situation. Daddy Lin writhed on the floor trying to break his bonds.

Nathan bit his bottom lip. He looked to the men in the jail, then to Daddy Lin. Glancing back to the men, Nathan weighed the consequences of speaking over consoling his Daddy Lin. In the end, his loyalty won out and Nathan drew on his training and love for Daddy Lin. Nathan had to be brave. His Daddy Lin needed him.

"It's okay," Nathan's voice was barely over a whisper. He watched Daddy Lin for some sort of recognition. When Daddy Lin continued to struggle, Nathan swallowed his fear down and said louder. "Daddy Lin, it'll be okay." Nathan sighed when Daddy Lin stopped struggling and angled his head so he could see Nathan. "Daddy Lin." Nathan reached for the bars.

"Hey, kid." Nathan froze when he heard one of the men from the cell call out to him. "Hey, kid, can you get out?"

Nathan swallowed hard. He kept his eyes on Daddy Lin who did his best to nod to answer the man. "No," Nathan lied, shaking his head emphatically. He never disobeyed Daddy Lin on purpose, but the truth was he mentally couldn't escape this cage.

The man sighed, "It's okay. Once the people at the camp realize we haven't arrived, I'm sure they'll come looking for us."

"They are a bunch of young boys. What are they going to do?" one of the other men grumbled.

Nathan brightened. Ryan! Ryan who had found him and came to visit him lived at the camp. He played video games with Nathan and made him laugh with

his funny stories about his friends. When Daddy Lin told him he wanted Nathan to talk to someone, Ryan was there and held his hand. He told Nathan he'd always be there for him.

"Fuck, we'll probably be dead by the time they get here," snorted the other man.

The door to the playroom opened and they all grew quiet. Nathan huddled in the back of the cage, keeping his eyes on Daddy Lin. Corbin came into view first, then the scary, muscly man, Rafi. They stood on either side of Daddy Lin. Corbin squatted down and removed the gag from Daddy Lin's mouth.

"You going to talk now bitch?" he said with a sneer.

"Fuck you," Daddy Lin said working his jaw. "I told you there's no money here."

Rafi leaned down, putting a knee in the small of Daddy Lin's back. "You better be lying because if that's true, then there's no reason to keep your punk ass around."

"Walden probably didn't have a chance to tell him. He did die before he got here." Corbin slowly turned his head toward Nathan. "That one, though. He knows."

Rafi stood, annoyance on his face. "Fuck, Corbin! Why are we fucking with this bitch, then? Why aren't we trying to get that little brat to talk?!"

"Leave him alone," Daddy Lin said with the bite of a toothless dog.

"Because he doesn't talk." Corbin came over to the cage. Nathan pressed himself as far back into the corner as he could. "He's fucked up. We need that one to get this one to talk."

The mean muscle man came over to the cage. "Oh, I can get him to talk."

Nathan's eyes grew wide with fear. Rafi reached into the cage and grabbed Nathan by the ankle. Nathan let out a high pitched shriek and began kicking at the man until he let go. He continued screaming while the two men covered their ears and moved away from the cage.

Corbin punched Rafi in the arm. "That's why, Rafi. Fuck, man. Would you listen?"

"Hit me again and see what happens," Rafi warned. "Come on, we got to find that money before someone else comes snooping around." Rafi stopped in front of Daddy Lin. "You better convince your screaming banshee of a boy to tell you where that money is before I have to." He punctuated the statement with a kick into Daddy Lin's stomach.

When he heard the door to the playroom shut, Nathan inched his way over toward the edge of the cage "Daddy Lin?" he asked meekly. "Daddy Lin, are you okay?"

"Yeah, I'm fine," Daddy Lin groaned. Nathan watched Daddy Lin contort his body so he could see Nathan. "I need you to be brave for my friends." Nathan hugged himself. "Those men in the cell, that one is my friend Josh. Those other two men are his friends. They are good people. Say hello, Josh."

"Hi," Nathan heard from the cell, but kept his eyes on Daddy Lin.

"Josh, this is Nathan." Daddy Lin kept his eyes on Nathan as he spoke. "He's the special young man I told you about."

"Oh, hi, Nathan. Your Daddy Lin has told me a lot about you." Josh spoke with a soft cautious tone, like he was speaking to a scared animal. "I was looking forward to meeting you. I just wish the circumstances were better."

"Nathan, remember your manners," Daddy Lin gently scolded.

"H-hi, Mister Josh." The words stumbled out of Nathan's mouth.

Daddy Lin smiled. "Josh there knows a lot of funny stories. Would you like him to tell you a funny story?" Nathan nodded. "Ask him to tell you a funny story."

Nathan struggled to form the words. It took him a moment but he was finally able to say, "Mister Josh, will you please tell me a funny story?"

"We're locked in a cell about to die, and you're going to tell some freak boy a funny story?" groaned one of the other men.

Nathan winced at the hardness in his voice. He heard harsh whispers being exchanged between the men, but he kept his eyes on Daddy Lin who looked pleadingly at Nathan. If he could only get to his Daddy Lin and free him. Daddy Lin would know what to do. Daddy Lin would take him to someplace safe, away from these strangers and mean men.

"I'm sorry about that Nathan," Mister Josh said from the cell. "I'd love to tell you a funny story. Do you think you could look at me while I tell it?" Nathan saw his Daddy Lin nod to him to do it. Slowly he turned in the cage to face the men in the cell. "That's better. My you are a beautiful young man. Do you know that?"

"No." Nathan shook his head emphatically. A coy smile crept across his face. "Daddy Lin thinks I am, though."

"Your Daddy Lin has great taste." Josh's words caused the smile on Nathan to brighten. "Well, this story is really funny. It involves my friend Lin, a drag queen, and a big-dick twink."

"Oh, my god. Will I ever live that down?" Daddy Lin sighed.

"No, now hush so I can tell Nathan the funny story," Josh laughed. Nathan liked his laugh; it was warm and friendly. "Now, your Daddy Lin and I were in a small town filming. We had just finished working and stayed an extra day to enjoy the nightlife." Nathan leaned forward, eager to hear the story.

"I will get you back for this," Daddy Lin mumbled.

"You look a little tied up at the moment," Josh teased. "Now, where was I? Oh, yes. So I was watching the show while Daddy Lin was making out with this big-dick twink ..."

10

YOU'RE AN ASSHOLE

CAMERON STIRRED WHEN he felt the weight of a body next to his and the slow dance of fingers in his hair. Rolling over and tossing an arm around the unknown person, he snuggled into the hard body. The hand moved down his neck to rub circles in the middle of his back. Cameron let out a soft sound of contentment.

"Come on, Chipmunk, it's time to wake up," a familiar voice drifted softly into his ears.

Cameron was about to murmur his protest when his eyes shot open and jumped from the bed. "What the fuck, dude?"

"I was just trying to wake you up." Carlos smiled sweetly at him.

Cameron hated that he liked the intimate touch. He hated that he found he was beginning to like Carlos. He had already dated a porn actor, and the entire world saw how *that* ended up. He wasn't going to make that mistake twice. If he did this, it was only going to be fun, and it would be over when they parted ways.

"Yeah, well, thanks," Cameron scowled, storming off into the bathroom.

He started dressing in the clothes Ryan dropped off. He was grateful for the items, but hoped his own things would show up soon. While they fit size-wise, their cut left much to be desired. The jean cut-off shorts barely reached his upper thigh, and the shirt hung barely low enough to cover his flat stomach.

He was debating putting on the dirty clothes he came in when Carlos asked from the bedroom, "Are you ready yet, Chipmunk?"

With a sigh, he called back, "Yeah." Stepping back into the bedroom, he saw Carlos's eyes grow wide, then amused. "What?" he huffed, seeing Carlos holding back laughter.

"You're a little too big for those shorts," Carlos chuckled, rolling off the bed.

Confused, Cameron looked down at himself. It didn't take him long to spot the source of Carlos's amusement. His dick had slipped down his left leg and was poking out the bottom of his shorts. "Fuck," he groaned in dismay.

"Here." Carlos tossed a tank top and gym shorts onto the bed.

Relieved, Cameron pulled off one set of borrowed clothes and pulled on the new. "Thank you. I guess I can return these to Ryan."

"You don't have to." Cameron looked up to see Carlos leering at him. "I like the shorts."

Cameron glowered at Carlos. "Fuck you."

"Not until after we shoot. Come on, I'm hungry." Carlos casually strode out of the room.

Cameron slipped on his shoes before chasing after him. "We're not shooting."

"We'll see," Carlos responded, heading out the front door.

Cameron got to the front door in time to see Carlos getting onto a four-wheeler. "We don't have a crew or a director. Hell, we don't even have a script."

"Get on." Carlos started the vehicle. Cameron reluctantly stepped down from the cabin and slipped behind Carlos. "Hold on tight." Cameron put his arms around Carlos. "Tighter." Cameron squeezed Carlos tighter. "Perfect." Carlos slowly moved the four-wheeler forward.

"You're an asshole." Cameron grumbled in his ear, but he kept his grip around Carlos tight, telling himself, *this is just for fun.*

They rode up the five-hundred-or-so feet back to the pool. A group of guys were laughing and having fun. One guy manning a grill had his back to them, the others were in or around the pool. Water exploded when a hurtling body curled into a ball and landed in the pool near the others.

They parked beside several other four-wheelers. Cameron barely removed his arms from around Carlos when he heard excited squeals. Ryan's lithe sun-kissed body came bursting from the pool gate in what appeared to be black swim briefs. Cameron mused that in a different world, they'd either be the best of friends or most bitter of enemies.

"You're finally here! How do you like my swimsuit?!" Ryan spun around, revealing to Cameron that his swim briefs were actually a thong. "Oh, did you need to borrow a suit or are you going nude like Carlos?"

"Probably nude," Cameron answered, sliding off the four-wheeler.

Ryan took his hand and pulled him toward the pool. "Well, you're going to see us nude when you film us, so I guess it's only fair," and before Cameron could correct him, Ryan yelled, "Hey, guys! This is Cameron, the one that's going to direct our movie!"

Cameron froze when four sets of eyes landed on him. Before he could say anything Carlos's hand clapped his back. "He's not directing. I am."

"What? If anyone here is directing, it's going to be me." Cameron blurted out. He turned and scowled at Carlos's beaming face. "You're an asshole. Do we even have a script?"

"That we do." Carlos puffed up his chest proudly.

"It's not one of those, 'oh look, young sexy boys in nature fucking' scripts is it?" Cameron watched Carlos deflate. Groaning, Cameron said, "Let me see it, and I'll see what I can do."

Cameron found himself being lifted up in the air. "I knew you'd do it, Chipmunk!"

"Okay, why do you call him Chipmunk?" Ryan asked with a slight giggle to his voice.

Carlos put Cameron down, but did not let him go. "Because he wants my nut between his cheeks."

Cameron gawked at Carlos while the others erupted into laughter. Hysterical, Ryan asked, "Which set of cheeks?"

"Both of them, duh," Carlos answered casually.

Cameron struggled in Carlos's grip. "I'm going to beat your ass."

"There's paddles in the play room!" called someone from behind Cameron.

Cameron glowered at Carlos who was holding back laughter. "You will pay for that," he threatened.

"How about I help choreograph the sex and eat your ass later?" Carlos ran his tongue over his lips.

Cameron rolled his eyes. "I was going to make you do that anyways."

"You don't have to make me do anything," Carlos said seductively. "All you have to do is ask."

"Down, boy. Save it for the camera." Cameron pushed himself away from Carlos.

"If you two are done flirting, I'd like to introduce Chip, err, Cameron to the boys." Ryan pulled Cameron away by the hand to the shirtless man cooking at the grill. "This is Brad. Brad, this is Cameron."

Cameron took in the broad man. He stood almost six foot tall with short dirty-blonde hair that was matted down with sweat. He was barrel-chested and not overly defined, but he had a good bit of muscle. He reminded Cameron of the stereotypical boy-next-door.

"How's it going?" he gave Cameron a nod before returning his attention back to the grill.

"Good," Cameron answered, but he got the hint Brad wasn't listening.

Ryan ushered Cameron away. With his voice lowered, he said, "He's not much of a talker, but he is a screamer."

Before Cameron could ask what he meant, they were already coming up to the other guys in the pool. Carlos had been perched, squatting on the edge talking to the three in the water, but stood and faced Cameron and Ryan when they approached. He was smiling arrogantly. Cameron found it both aggravating and arousing.

"I knew you couldn't stay away, Chipmunk." Carlos said playfully.

Cameron's response was a hand on Carlos chest and a slight push backwards. He watched Carlos's eyes grow wide with surprise when his body bent back and he was unable to right himself. His arms flailed wildly about. In a futile attempt to steady himself, he grabbed Cameron's arm.

Cameron let out a short-lived yelp before the two went crashing into the water. Submerged, their bodies tangled. Separating from each other, they burst through the surface. Carlos was laughing. Cameron was glaring.

"Asshole!" Cameron bellowed, pushing his wet hair from his face.

Carlos peeled off his wet tank top. Wringing it out over the water, he asked, "Is that your pet name for me or what you want to see?" Frustrated, Cameron splashed him. "Come on, hand over your shirt so it'll dry."

"Here," he said, handing over his shirt to Carlos who handed both shirts to an amused Ryan. He watched Carlos then slip out of his shorts and hand those over. "Here," Cameron repeated, passing over his own shorts.

Having handed those as well to Ryan, Carlos returned his attention to him. "Guys, this is Chipmunk,

I mean Cameron. Our director." Cameron narrowed his eyes at Carlos. "Cameron, this is Cody." Carlos indicated the short pit bull of a man. "Mitch." The tall brunette with a runner's build nodded at him. "And Dean." He had chestnut wavy hair and glasses.

It was Mitch who cast the first stone of doubt. "Do you even know how to direct?"

"Yes," Cameron half-lied. He'd directed several student films, been on set with Lexi, but he had never actually directed an adult film. "Not this type of film, but it's not really that different."

Carlos added, "He'll have me to help him."

"This is going to be a fucking waste of time," Mitch grumbled.

Cody splashed him. "What else do we have to do? This place is closed until—"

"Cameron!" Ryan interrupted, standing at the edge of the pool holding out a towel. "Do you want to go check if the airline called about your luggage?"

"Yeah." Cameron made his way to the stairs. He wasn't as worried about the clothes as his toiletries. His entire skin care routine was in those bags. One thing you didn't mess with was a gay man's skin care.

He heard Carlos pout behind him. "Awe, I like you in my clothes." Then he playfully added, "I like you out of them more."

Taking the towel from Ryan, he flipped his middle finger at Carlos. That started a round of horseplay with hoots and hollers from the other boys as they ribbed Carlos. Before he turned away, he caught Carlos's eye. He gave Cameron a quick wink before diving into the orgy of splashing bodies.

WHERE IS IT?

THE SOUND OF the opening playroom door caused the room to plummet into silence. Nathan stopped giggling and scurried into the far corner of his cage. Mister Josh stopped in the middle of his story. Daddy Lin shot Nathan a worried look before he turned his attention to Corbin entering the room.

Corbin looked at them disdainfully. "What's so fucking funny?" He waited a moment for an answer which wasn't coming. "Do you think this is some fucking game? Maybe I'll let Rafi kill one of you, and then you might take this shit seriously."

Nathan drew his knees up to his chest for protection. He watched Corbin skulk over to Daddy Lin. Squatting down beside Daddy Lin's head, he said, "Come on, Lin. Help me out here. Just tell me where it is, and we'll leave."

"Fuck you. I don't know what you're talking about," Daddy Lin spat out.

Corbin's face reddened with anger. "The fuck you don't," Corbin said and stood so he was looming over Daddy Lin. "Walden said he'd never let anyone take his precious treasure from this place, even in death. Now, where is it?!"

"You're crazy. Everything Walden had is tied up trying to keep the camp going," Daddy Lin shot back, heat filling his words.

There was venom in Corbin's next words. "You wouldn't be struggling to keep the camp open if you'd just let me run it instead of firing me."

"You were letting the camp fall apart because you were too busy pimping the strung-out boys you brought in for the guests," indignation dripping from Daddy Lin's voice.

Corbin let out a blood curdling scream of rage and annoyance, "Where is the fucking money he stashed?!"

"What happened to all the money you made pimping out the boys at the camp? Did it all go up your nose or in your arm?" Daddy Lin accused.

Nathan clutched his knees closer. He watched Corbin rear back his leg to kick Daddy Lin, but stopped mid-swing. "It cost me a lot of money to keep those boys doped up for all those fat fucks who came here." Corbin began pacing and shaking his fist. "I owe people money. A *lot* of money. They want it and they want it *now*." Nathan saw a crazed look in his eyes. "I want that money! Now!"

"Shit in one hand and want in the other, and see which one fills up first." That comment by Daddy Lin was rewarded with a kick. Daddy Lin wheezed out, "Fucking prick."

Corbin turned his cruel, manic glare at Nathan. "Maybe we should start torturing your little boy there." Nathan tried to push himself further into the corner. "Maybe hearing him scream will make you talk."

"Leave him alone," Daddy Lin coughed out.

Corbin turned his attention back to Daddy Lin. "You have until morning to tell us what we need, or I'm going to let Rafi have his way with that boy right in front of you."

"Touch him and you'll both regret it," Daddy Lin threatened.

Nathan watched Corbin kick Daddy Lin again and then leave. Fear made him contain his sobs. He knew exactly what those mean men were looking for. If he told them, they might leave like they said, but Nathan had been made promises by cruel men like that before. They never kept their promises.

12

INTRIGUED

CARLOS SLIPPED AWAY from the boys wrestling in the water to lean over the pool edge. He watched Ryan and Cameron walk up the path to the main office. He couldn't explain it. From the moment he saw the slender young man soaping himself in the shower, Carlos wanted him … and not just for his body. There was something about the way he moved. And when Carlos looked into his eyes, he was hooked.

"You like him, huh?" Mitch asked, swimming up next to him.

"No," Carlos said, keeping his eyes on Cameron and the slight hip bump of his walk. "I'm intrigued."

Mitch shoulder bumped Carlos. "Like Cody is intrigued with Brad?"

Carlos looked over at the grill where Cody had joined Brad. Cody's five-foot-five height was dwarfed even more by Brad's six-foot-three. "They would make an odd, but cute couple," Carlos mused. "I was only here a day and thought they were together by how they acted with each other."

"I still can't believe they haven't fucked yet," Mitch laughed softly. "I'm surprised they agreed to do this movie."

Carlos turned his attention back up toward Cameron and Ryan. "Why did you?"

"So I could have sex with hot guys like you," Mitch teased. "No, but seriously. We knew the camp was in trouble before Ryan told us. We like it here, and Lin did right by us after he got rid of that bastard Corbin." Mitch moved to hug Carlos from behind. Resting his head on Carlos's shoulder, he continued. "That's why we started posting on fan sites and giving the money to Lin. This is our home."

"I get that. Every time I think I have a home, a place to lay my head down, I'm back looking for another place," Carlos sighed.

Mitch gave Carlos a slight squeeze. "You could always stay here with us. Brad and Cody are working on a way to get us internet lines run down here. Soon, we'll be streaming live shows from the woods."

"I wish I could, but I think I want to go to school. Learn more about film making, you know?" Carlos pushed away from the edge and out of Mitch's arms. "I know I can do more than just have sex on camera."

Mitch splashed him. "Is that why you conned Cameron into filming without a director?"

"Yup," Carlos smiled. *That and I didn't want him to leave.*

Mitch splashed him again. "Don't forget about us when you're a big hot-shot director."

"I won't," Carlos laughed, splashing back. "I think I might want to create my own studio, my own brand."

Dean appeared on the pool edge. The bright red trunks he wore obscenely clung to his package. Sitting down and dangling his legs in the water, he said, "I went to take a piss in the woods and heard something."

"Your dick hitting the ground when you pulled it out?" Mitch joked.

Dean kicked water at him. "My dick isn't *that* big."

"Dude you can check someone's tonsils through their ass," Mitch continued.

Dean rolled his eyes. "Anyways, I was pissing in the bushes over there, and I heard someone or something moving in the woods. I thought it was one of you, but when I looked back, you all were still at the pool."

"Ooo, scary," Mitch mocked. "We have some sort of serial killer in the woods."

Carlos grew serious. "Not funny. I told you what happened with Dennis and my friend, Billy. It would be my luck."

"I think we should buddy-up tonight, and double check our locks." Carlos heard the trepidation in Dean's voice.

Mitch let out a playful sigh. "The things you'll say to get me in your bed."

"Fuck you. I was going to bunk with Ryan," Dean lightheartedly jabbed back.

Carlos looked back down the trail Ryan and Cameron disappeared into. Breaking the levity, he asked, "Do you think they'll be okay?" Carlos heard

both boys erupt into laughter. Confused by their amusement, he looked back at them for a clue.

"Are you kidding?" Dean asked between chortles.

Carlos looked to Mitch for an explanation. It took him a moment to remember Carlos was new. "Ryan is the bouncer here. If he doesn't cut you down with his words, he'll do it with his fists."

"When that ass, Corbin, came back to try and shake us down for money, Ryan had him pinned on the ground begging for mercy," Dean added in.

Worried, Carlos looked back down the trail while Mitch and Dean continued recounting Ryan's exploits. He didn't have a good feeling about this. If only they had cell service down here, he'd feel slightly better. All he needed was for this shoot to turn into a slasher flick.

13

I KNOW WHO YOU ARE

CAMERON AND RYAN walked in silence to the office. The sun was setting behind them. Ryan kept looking back like he was expecting someone to follow them. Every time he turned his head back, the grin on his face got bigger and bigger. Cameron looked back once or twice, but all he saw were the boys playing in the pool.

"Why do you keep looking back?" Cameron finally asked.

Ryan let out a soft chuckle. "One of us has an admirer, and it isn't me."

"What are you talking about?" Cameron asked, confusion on his face.

Ryan stopped mid-stride. Putting his hands on his hips, he said, "Honey, you can't be *that* oblivious." Cameron motioned with his hands and head for Ryan to explain further. "Carlos. He has it bad for you."

"Oh, that," Cameron brushed off, starting to walk again. "That's just fun. Nothing more. I don't date porn actors."

"Just get engaged to them." Cameron froze at Ryan's retort. "I know who you are. Just because we don't have internet at the camp, doesn't mean we don't go online."

"Who else knows?" Cameron asked, voice soft and filled with dread.

With an air of indifference, Ryan sashayed past him saying, "Just me."

"Please, don't tell anyone," Cameron pleaded, breaking into a brief jog to catch up to Ryan. "One of the reasons I'm here is to let all that die down."

Cameron didn't like the glint in Ryan's eye when Ryan turned his head to talk. "I will, on three conditions."

"You're blackmailing me?" Cameron gawked.

Ryan waved his hand dismissively. "Blackmail is an ugly word. We're just bargaining to keep your secret."

"Blackmail," Cameron clarified.

Ryan exhaled hotly. "Fine blackmail, but I don't think you'll mind my conditions."

"Get on with it already," Cameron groaned.

Ryan held up a finger. "One, we do my rewrite of the script instead of that lame-ass canned dialogue they sent."

"Okay, I don't care what we film. Hell, I didn't want to film to begin with," Cameron shrugged.

Ryan held up a second finger. "Two, you give Carlos a fair chance."

"I thought you were my friend," Cameron feigned mock indignation.

Ryan put a hand on his shoulder. "I know you're bitter–"

"I am *not* bitter," Cameron defended.

"And I'm not a fem power top," Ryan quipped back. "Anyways, I consider myself a good judge of character, and Carlos is a good guy. In the short time he's been here, he's really connected and bonded with all of us." Cameron let those words sink in. "Maybe you should try to get to know him … other than carnally, that is. I know that'll be hard—pun intended—but try."

Cameron laughed. "Hard is an understatement. He drives me mad, but I sort of enjoy it."

"Just talk to him. You'd be surprised by the man underneath." Ryan gave Cameron's shoulder a squeeze before withdrawing.

They walked in silence for a time when Cameron realized Ryan had only given him two conditions. "Wait, what's the third condition?"

"How could I forget?" Dramatically, Ryan put his hands up, fingers splayed. "I want an autographed picture of your aunt, Sexy Lexi Luscious!"

Cameron burst out into laughter. "It's just Lexi Luscious."

"No, honey, it's Sexy Lexi Luscious. Trust me," Ryan corrected. "She's a badass. Did you know she broke the nose of a three-hundred-pound biker who was rude to her?"

Cameron couldn't hold back the laughter. "Actually, it was two three-hundred-pound bikers, and they

were hitting on her and not taking no for an answer. At least that's what she told me when I bailed her out."

"Fabulous," Ryan said with pride and awe. "She's the reason I started training in different forms of defense."

"Like you need it around here," Cameron teased.

Ryan's voice grew somber. "Actually, yes. This place has a dark history."

"Oh?"

"You're going to find out anyway, so let me give you the real tea." They stopped in front of the office. Ryan knelt down, pulled a key from under a flower pot and opened the door. He stepped in and turned on the lights, Cameron on his heels. "I already know the airline hasn't called. I checked right before we went down for dinner."

Questioningly, Cameron looked at Ryan. "Then why did we come up here?"

"Girl talk." Ryan plopped down on the beat up couch they had in the office for guests while they waited. "I wanted to get you alone to talk, and that boy in your cabin wasn't going to leave you alone." Ryan patted the seat beside him. "Sit. Let's have a Kiki."

"Shit!" Cameron exclaimed, feeling like he was falling through the couch as he sank down.

Ryan laughed. "I know we need a new one, but there's no money for it. All the money we make is for renovating the cabins."

"You know, this place has a lot of potential even without the internet," Cameron said, struggling to situate himself in the broken couch.

There was a wistful air of nostalgia in Ryan's voice when he spoke next. "I started working here when I was just eighteen. I used to clean the cabins and occasionally the Fort. Back then, Walden ran this place. He was strict about employees not fraternizing with the guests." Cameron listened, not wanting to interrupt. "We had this one guest who mistook this place for one of those kink camps."

Ryan shuddered. "He always placed the 'Do Not Disturb' sign on his door, which suited me just fine. He was one of those creepy types who kept leering at the employees and grabbing us. Walden caught wind of it and told the man to stop or get out. He begrudgingly agreed. Then, he lectured us that if anyone touched us inappropriately, we were to report it immediately. He wasn't tolerating that shit."

Ryan took a moment to gather his words. "I was making my rounds and saw some kid run out of his cabin. I didn't think anything of it at the time." The somberness returned to Ryan's voice. "I was cleaning the cabin next to his when he got back and went ballistic."

Cameron noticed Ryan was staring out into space rather than looking at him. "He kept screaming, 'Where is he? Where is he?' I went over to see what the matter was. The dude was a mad man. Have you ever see someone with that crazed look in their eyes? Trust me, you don't ever want to see it directed at you."

Ryan closed his eyes and hugged himself. "He screamed at me that *I* had stolen his property and he wanted his boy back, and if we didn't give him back

he'd take me instead. He lunged at me and grabbed my arm to keep me from running away."

Cameron put a hand on Ryan's knee. "Oh, my God, what happened?"

"Luckily someone saw me go into his cabin," Ryan exhaled the weight of the story. "Walden came bursting in with two of our bigger employees. They got into a shouting match about me and the boy who wasn't there. The man let go of my arm and they took the man away from me. I bolted out of that cabin.

"The entire camp was there. You know gossip and drama travel faster than the speed of light with the gays." Ryan finally looked at Cameron. "I know the cops were called, and the man was taken away in cuffs. He had a few outstanding warrants and was trying to hide here. After it was all done, I told Walden about the boy I saw running from the cabin."

"What happened to the boy?" Cameron asked.

Ryan gave a little smile. "Nathan. His name is Nathan. Walden took him in, eventually. I saw him scavenging around the camp, eating out of the gar-bage cans and such. Anytime I tried to get near him, he'd turn and run into the woods. So, I started leaving food and clothes out for him. It took a week or so, but one day I was sitting on a picnic table when he came up and sat beside me. We just sat there, not saying anything when he said in this soft, almost broke voice, 'thank you.'"

"What happened then?"

Ryan smiled warmly. "I had already talked to Walden about letting him sleep in one of the cabins. He was skittish at first. I had to promise he'd be safe,

and that I'd come to see him every day. I eventually got him to meet Walden." Ryan shifted on the couch. "Walden fell in love with Nathan the moment he saw him. Not in a sexual way. More like a son, and he eventually moved in with Walden."

"Is he still . . ." Cameron didn't know how to finish the question.

"I would go over and play video games with him and tell him stories about the camp." Ryan pulled his legs up on the couch and sat crossed-legged. "He eventually told us his story. He had aged out of the foster system. He was struggling to survive when he met that guy on one of those apps. The first time they met, he locked Nathan in a cage for three days until Nathan promised to be his sex slave. He took all of Nathan's clothes and basically held him hostage."

Ryan sighed. "Taking care of Nathan took up a lot of Walden's time. He became the father Nathan never had. Nathan needed him and Walden needed Nathan. That's when he turned over day-to-day operations to that bastard, Corbin."

"What was so bad about Corbin?"

Ryan looked at Cameron as if he should know. "He ran off all the good people. Well, everyone but me. He started bringing in these young boys who were barely eighteen. I'm not sure where he found them, but they'd be addicted to one thing or another. Those guys down there were the exceptions."

"What was the point in hiring drug addicts?"

Ryan put a hand on Cameron's knee. "Honey, if you're itching for a fix, you'll suck any dick you're told."

Cameron nodded. "Gotcha."

"Corbin tried to keep me away from Walden and Nathan. I didn't get to see them as often as previously, but I did sometimes. That's why I didn't know he was sick. Had I known …" Ryan teared up. "No. No tears," he pronounced. "We didn't know this, but Walden had already contacted Lin to take over running the camp. Lin was staying in the camp to get a feel for it when Walden passed away in his sleep from a heart attack." Ryan took in a deep breath. "Lin helped me kick Corbin out, get what boys who hadn't disappeared into treatment, and I helped Nathan get accustomed to Lin."

"Wow, that's a lot." Cameron shook his head, ashamed to be upset because everyone saw his break up. "When do I get to meet Lin? It would be nice to meet the owner before we shoot."

The cackle of delight from Ryan threw Cameron off. "Honey, you've already met him. Walden left his place to me. Well, me and Nathan. Lin is just the face of the camp. Oh, and Nathan's boyfriend."

"Wait, I was under the impression Lin was the owner," Cameron explained, confused.

Ryan squeezed his knee. "And we would like the general public to keep thinking that way. He's the face, I'm the brains."

"But—"

"Honey, would you go to a big ol' roughing-it-camp run by me?" Ryan fluttered his eyes. "Or a big strapping, muscly man with the tightest ass you'd love to sink your cock into?"

"True," Cameron paused, realizing what Ryan said. "Wait. Are *you* fucking Lin?"

"No!" Ryan answered, offended.

"What about Nathan?"

Ryan waived his hand in dismissal. "Oh, no. I don't fuck him, but he fucks Lin. I walked in on them once. Hot."

"So you own this place," Cameron recounted, ignoring the last comment.

"Correct."

"And Nathan is fucking Lin."

"Correct." Ryan's eyes narrowed when he saw the deviousness in Cameron's eyes. "Go ahead, tell everyone. I don't have anything to lose."

"Fuck." Cameron pounded the couch with one hand. "Anyway, how is Nathan?"

"Aside from refusing to wear clothes, and a debilitating fear of people? Great." Ryan smiled. "Your turn. Tell me about this break up."

Cameron groaned, "As if you haven't seen it all over the internet."

"That was a video of what happened. I want the play-by-play of what led up to that." Ryan leaned forward, interested. "Give me the skinny, you skinny bitch."

Cameron couldn't help but smile. "Okay, truth was, I was thinking of calling it off for a while. Alex was nice when I met him, but he grew more arrogant and shady as his popularity grew. We had this understanding that off camera we were exclusive. I mean, he *is* a porn actor."

"Right," Ryan chimed in.

"I caught him cheating twice. He said he was auditioning people for content, and I believed him."

Cameron rolled his eyes. "I kept hearing whispers and rumors about him cheating on me, and I ignored them. Then he saw this guy Billy at my aunt's party, and Alex just bolted over to him. Words were exchanged, and Billy let loose the bomb that Alex was trying to date this guy Dennis on the side."

"Dennis?" Ryan asked cautiously. "Not the one who was kidnapped?"

"Yeah."

Ryan thought for a moment. "Didn't that boy Billy almost get killed the next day by an old lover?"

"Yeah, I was hoping that would stop the buzz about my break up, but it reignited it." Cameron fell back in to the couch. "Hey, can I use the office phone to call my aunt?"

Ryan nodded. "Go right ahead."

With a little help, Cameron got up. Putting the phone to his ear, he turned it on and off again. "The line is dead."

"Don't be saying that scary movie bullshit." Ryan got up. Taking the phone and hearing for himself, he said. "It is. That's odd. I'll have Cody look at it tomorrow."

"I'll just ride up to the main road in the morning and call her from my cell," Cameron shrugged. "Shall we head back?"

"Sure." Cameron could tell that Ryan was holding something back. "Let's go enjoy the night before the fireworks."

"Fireworks?"

14

PILLOW TALK

CAMERON HUNG THEIR wet things to dry on the towel rack in the bathroom. He turned the shower on, wanting to wash off the residue of the night. He was outside the shower, leaning in to test the water temperature, when an all-too-familiar body pressed against his back and hands wrapped around his waist.

"Mind if I join you?" Carlos purred in his ear.

Of course he didn't mind. He had expected Carlos to join him in the shower. He wanted Carlos to join him. Of course, he couldn't tell Carlos that, though he probably already knew. The question was more formality, part of their cat-and-mouse game.

When Cameron got back to the pool with Ryan, he and Carlos found every excuse to casually touch each other. It started out small: a hand on a shoulder, or on the small of a back. It progressed to Carlos holding him from behind and him draping Carlos around him like a warm blanket.

"Fine, but keep *him* under control," Cameron teased, bumping his butt back into Carlos's hard cock.

Carlos pulled Cameron flush against him. "But he likes you, Chipmunk."

"You have a shoot tomorrow," Cameron chided, pulling away and stepping into the shower.

Carlos stepped in behind him and huffed, "I know Chipmunk."

"And stop calling me Chipmunk," Cameron griped playfully.

Carlos put his hands on Cameron's hips. "Yes, Chipmunk."

The shower was sensual and teasing. As they took turns using the mesh body sponge to spread soap over each other, their faces came so close. Cameron thought Carlos might actually kiss him, but he restrained himself, even as their hard cocks battered each other's legs.

As they were drying off, Cameron knew he had to ward off the inevitable. "Shorts." Carlos looked at him questioningly. "We need shorts for bed, and you're staying on *your* side of the bed."

"Fine," Carlos pouted, slinking into the bedroom. "Only because I have to film."

Cameron followed, catching a pair of shorts Carlos threw at him. "It's for the—why are you not putting on shorts?" he asked when Carlos slipped into the bed naked.

"I assumed you meant you," Carlos grinned, putting his hand behind his head. "I can control myself, Chipmunk."

Cameron threw the shorts back at Carlos. "I meant *both* of us." Cameron went over to the dresser and pulled out another pair of running shorts.

"Can I at least eat your booty before we go to bed?" Carlos whined, slipping the shorts on under the covers.

Cameron was tempted, but he knew it wouldn't stop there. "No."

"Aw, come on." Cameron didn't like the silliness in Carlos's voice. "It's supposed to be eaten."

"No," Cameron said firmly, going to the other side of the bed. He knew he was going to regret it, but he still asked, "Why is it supposed to be eaten?"

"A booty is supposed to be eaten because it's cut in half," Carlos laughed. "No! Wait! It's because it's between two buns!"

Cameron gaped at him. Getting into the bed, he shook his head. "Why are you like this?"

"You just bring it out in me." Carlos turned out the lights. "Hey, Chipmunk. I promise to stay on my side of the bed, but you're more than welcome to come over and pay a visit if you get lonely."

Cameron shuffled over in the bed. "If it'll keep you quiet." Laying his head on Carlos's chest and draping his arm over his waist, Cameron said, "Now, go to sleep."

"Okay," Carlos said with a kiss on the top of Cameron's head. "This is nice, just holding someone while you fall asleep. I haven't done something like this since I moved out of my friend Billy's place."

Cameron stiffened at that name. He asked, "Billy?"

"Yeah, we met in a bar when I was on the streets hustling after my family kicked me out." Carlos began slowly stroking Cameron's back.

"Why did your family kick you out?" Cameron asked, already knowing the answer.

Carlos spoke as if it didn't bother him, but Cameron heard it in his voice when he answered, "Because I like to kiss boys."

"Oh." Cameron wasn't sure what to say. His own parents had died when he was discovering his sexuality, and Aunt Lexi was so open and loving that he never had to worry about that. "Were you and Billy a thing?"

Carlos took in a deep breath and exhaled slowly. "No, I mean we used to fuck on camera, but we were friends, not lovers. I used to see Billy in passing. We'd chit-chat, nothing major. Then one day he came up to me and asked me how much for the whole night," Carlos laughed. "I thought he was fucking with me, so I told him a thousand."

"What did he do?" Cameron was running his finger around Carlos's belly button.

Carlos's chest bounced with a tiny laugh. "He gave it to me and we went back to his place. He told me to go shower, and when I came out he had food for us. Then we played video games all night long."

"He didn't want anything from you?"

Cameron heard the smile in Carlos's voice. "If you met Billy, you'd understand. The only thing he ever wants from someone is their friendship. He never wants to hurt his friends. That's why he found me a place to live before he moved out west, and why he

86

told my manager Hunter instead of Dennis about that dude … what's his name?"

"Alex." Cameron bit the inside of his lip when he said the name.

Carlos snuggled closer to Cameron. "Yeah, Alex. How did you know that name?"

"It's a small world in porn," Cameron answered vaguely. Needing to change the subject, Cameron asked, "Is this what you want to do with your life?"

Carlos pulled Cameron close. "No, porn is just what I fell into to make ends meet. I think I want to go back to school for film."

"Directing?"

Carlos yawned, "Maybe. I guess I'll find out when I start school."

"You know we have some great schools out west," Cameron said hopefully.

Carlos snorted with a big yawn. "I guess I could crash with Billy and his boyfriend, Jordan, for a bit." He patted Cameron on the back. "Let's get some sleep, okay?"

Cameron closed his eyes and listened to the rhythmic beating of Carlos's heart. "Okay. Good night, Carlos."

"Good night, Chipmunk."

15

I CAN DO THIS

NATHAN LAY ON the mat in his cage pretending to sleep, trying to formulate a plan. He knew he could get out. Corbin and Rafi hadn't been back for some time, so it had to be night. He could hear Daddy Lin breathing deeply and the soft snores of the men in the cage. He knew he could get them out. He just had to get the master key from inside the house.

He felt guilty for lying earlier, but the cage he couldn't get out of wasn't the one with bars. He was ready now. He was terrified, but ready. He needed to make that fear drive him into action instead of crippling him.

He could hear his therapist's voice in his head. *Fear can either cripple you or drive you into action. You get to decide which.*

Fear had driven him to trek through the forest and rush out into the camp to find Ryan. Now he had to use fear to save Daddy Lin and his friends. He had to use that fear to keep Rafi from going to the camp and hurting Ryan. He could do it. He did it before.

Checking to see if everyone was still asleep, Nathan took a deep breath. He pulled up the left corner of the mat. There, dulled by time, was the metal key to his cage. Gingerly picking up the key with two fingers he laid the mat back down. Clutching the prize to his chest, he exhaled.

He checked once more to make sure everyone was sleeping. He took several deep calming breaths. He slipped his hands through the bars and began feeling around for the key hole. He almost dropped the key with the excitement of finding it.

He carefully pushed the key into the lock. Turning it, he heard the click of the lock opening. It was a soft sound, but sounded like thunder to Nathan's ears. He opened the cage door slowly, carefully. He looked to his bound Daddy Lin, then to the men in the cage. They were still sleeping.

Tentatively, he put out his left hand and then his right. Slowly he pulled himself out of the cage, mindful of any sound. Pulling himself from the cage, he turned around and quietly shut the cage door. Locking it back, he reached back into the cage and hid the key back under the mat.

He looked at his Daddy Lin, just a few feet away. How Nathan longed to snuggle up next to him, but he knew he couldn't. If he woke Daddy Lin, he'd order Nathan not to do what he was about to do. Daddy Lin wouldn't understand. He had no choice. This was the only way he could rescue Daddy Lin and his friends.

He had to sneak into the house and get that master key. No matter what.

Standing up, his joints and muscles ached from hunching over in the cage for so long. He twisted, stretching his knotted body. He took a deep breath. Letting it out slowly, he took that first cautious step, then the next. Making his way to the playroom door without making a sound, he slowly turned the knob.

Nathan was hit with the warm fresh air as it poured through the door. Crickets filled the night with the sound of their chirping. The moon, full and high in the sky, cast the only light. Nathan could see Daddy Lin's truck between him and the house. Two cars Nathan did not recognize were parked behind him.

Nathan took another steadying breath before stepping out into the darkness. Gingerly he shut the door behind him before taking his first steps alone into the night. Each wary step he took he expected one of the two men to come jumping out at him. He would bury that fear, then take another step.

His heart raced as he made it to the front door. He took two deep breaths. *It's now or never.* He didn't remember putting his hand on the knob. He turned it, but it did not move. He almost screamed. *Of course they locked it!* He clenched his hands into fists. *The back door!*

Nathan made the treacherous trek around the house, ducking under windows and listening for any other footsteps. It felt like an eternity before he made it. *Please*, he prayed, trying the knob. *Stupid! Stupid! Stupid!* Nathan mentally berated himself as this knob also refused to move. He was ready to lay there on the

back porch, let the men find him and do what they wanted with him.

No. Standing up straight and throwing his shoulders back, Nathan refused to give in. *I did it once. I can do it again.*

He stepped off the porch and headed toward the woods. Pushing his way through the brush, he found what he was looking for. It had grown over a bit, but he found the trail Ryan used to come visit. Nathan used it once before. They never expected him to actually need it again.

With only the filtered light of the moon through the trees by which to see, Nathan started down the path. *You can do this. You can,* he told himself over and over again, doing his best not to panic. *Do this for Daddy Lin. Do this for Ryan,* he encouraged himself. *I can do this.*

Nathan took a deep breath and trudged on. *I have to warn Ryan. I have to save Daddy Lin and his friends. I have to.* Heading into the darkness of the trail, he pushed down the fear. *I can be brave.*

16

LET'S MAKE A FUCKING MOVIE

CAMERON WAS A bit concerned after speaking to his Aunt Lexi. He told her about the director and his crew not showing up and their plans to go ahead with shooting the film. She gave him her blessings, but was worried about Josh and his crew not showing up because that wasn't like him at all.

"I'll make some calls, make sure everything is okay," she told him. There was a pause. "Alex called me. He asked if he could have more time to move out of the condo."

Cameron bit his tongue. "How much more time?"

"Six months," Lexi had hesitantly answered. "He's got a full schedule of shooting and doesn't have time to look, or so he claims."

Cameron quelled the anger. "Tell him he has three, and we'll be formalizing that in writing."

"I figured." He could hear Lexi's smile over the phone. "I'll have the papers drafted and sent over first thing in the morning."

"Thank you."

"You sound different." There was a brief pause between them. When Cameron didn't answer the unspoken question, she said, "Anyways, good luck in filming. I can help you edit the footage when you get back."

"I love you," Cameron answered, debating on telling her about Carlos. In the end, he didn't. After this shoot, he doubted he'd ever see the Latin lover again. "I need to head back to camp."

His next call was to the airline who still hadn't located his luggage. Doing his best not to yell and scream at the poor underpaid person taking his call, he thanked them and hung up. He'd have to continue wearing Carlos's clothes, which wasn't a bad thing. They smelled like him, innocent and spicy.

Back at the camp, he parked at the pool and headed toward the kitchen. Ryan did all the hard work, finding the locations for the shoot, pairing up the boys and getting them copies of the new scripts. When he entered the kitchen, they were all sitting around different tables practicing their lines together. Carlos was going from table to table helping them and giving them tips and tricks.

"Is everyone ready?" Cameron asked loud enough to get everyone's attention. With everyone's eyes on him, Cameron asked, "Does everyone know their parts?"

When no one answered, Carlos spoke up, "They are getting there."

"Good." Cameron wasn't sure what to say next so he said the first thing that came to mind. "Let's make

a fucking film." That earned him some laughter, and he felt more at ease. "I know you guys have fucked on camera before, but this is going to be different. Try not to ad lib, and Carlos will be helping direct the sex."

"So, he's going to tell us how to fuck?" Dean asked, trying to be funny. "Can we see his credentials? Get some references?"

Carlos dropped his shorts. "Here's my credentials." He nodded over to Cameron. "He's my reference."

"To be fair, we haven't fucked." The room filled with "oohs" and "ahhs" to Cameron's comment. "And if we don't start shooting soon, you'll never get that honor, Latin lover."

Carlos pulled his pants back up. "You heard the man, let's get to work so I can get me some Chipmunk cheeks."

"Stop calling me Chipmunk," Cameron groaned.

Carlos winked at him. "Anything you say, Chipmunk."

"His scenes are last, right, Ryan?" Cameron asked, glaring at Carlos.

Ryan let out an over exaggerated sigh. "I can move them to the front of the line if it means the two of you will finally fuck and stop this annoying flirting."

"No, we'll keep the schedule as is." Carlos gave Cameron a crooked smile. "I want to make Chipmunk wait."

"Let's go guys." Ryan stood. "The sooner we get your scenes shot, the sooner we can film Carlos's and this," Ryan waved his hand between Carlos and Cameron, "whatever this is will be over."

Cameron was impressed by how Carlos went from silly to professional once they started actually working. The first scene wasn't sex at all. It was the boys arriving at the camp. Ryan decided on using their Barracks since there weren't any other cabins around. It took about thirty minutes for them to get all the angles and lighting right.

Using tripods, they set cameras all around with Cameron using the manual camera and Ryan using the boom microphone. Everyone knew their lines and said them so naturally Cameron had to check the script to make sure they were saying the right ones.

That part went so smoothly they decided to go ahead with the cabin scene. The boys tossed their backpacks stuffed with their clothes onto the floor. Cody and Brad announced they wanted to check out the trails. Carlos said he wanted to take a nap. Dean said he wanted to shower off the grime of the road trip, while Mitch said he wanted to explore the camp.

Ryan wasn't in this scene. His first scene was with Carlos in a tent in the woods. Cameron wasn't sure how he felt about that. This was Carlos's job after all, and he knew Ryan knew the complicated situation between him and Carlos. He knew this, but it still felt weird. When he was on set with Alex, it never bothered him.

That should have been my first clue, Cameron chided himself while they set up in the woods. "Dean, I want you taking the shot of them walking up close. We'll use your height. Carlos, you guide him. Ryan you're on sound again. Mitch, I want you over here, taking the shot from a distance. Cody and Brad, are you ready?"

Cameron saw the nervous look of fear in their faces. He looked at Carlos. He had never been an adult film actor. The only times he had been filmed having sex were private sex videos he made sure were permanently deleted when the relationships ended.

"Brad, come over here for a second," Carlos ordered. "Cody, you go talk to Cameron."

Cameron mentally cursed as the squat man came over to him. He and Brad were dressed similarly in tight shorts and tank tops which showed off their sculpted physiques. With their rugged boyish looks, they would have had their pick of any man or woman in California.

Putting an arm around Cody's shoulder, Cameron guided him away from the others. "Look, I've never had sex on camera like this," he said once they were out of earshot. "I know it can be scary your first time, or so I am told."

"It's not that." Cody looked back over his shoulder at Brad.

It took Cameron a moment to realize the problem. "Oh. The fact you've got feelings for Brad?"

"You know?" Cody asked, exasperated.

Cameron rubbed Cody's broad back. "Everyone does. I think that's why Ryan put you two together in this scene."

"He's an ass," Cody grumbled. "He knows how bad I want Brad."

Cameron had an idea. "I've bet you've fantasized about what you'd like to do to him."

"Yeah."

Cameron smiled. "I want you to use that. Make your fantasy a reality. Use this scene to show him how you feel about him. Do you think you can do that?"

"Maybe," Cody shrugged.

Cameron rolled his eyes. "Fine. If you can't film this scene with Brad, I'll swap you out with Mitch or Dean."

"Fuck that." Cody's eyes flared with jealousy. "Okay, let's do this."

They made their way back to the others about the same time as Carlos and Brad. Carlos headed straight to Cameron, smiling ear to ear. Brad and Cody went to their places, waiting for direction. Cameron looked at Brad. He looked as if he had a similar change to Cody.

"Everything good?" he asked Carlos.

"Yeah," Carlos answered. "I just had to threaten to swap him out for Dean or Mitch."

Cameron laughed, "That's what I did."

"Great minds," Carlos snickered.

Cameron brushed past Carlos. "Come on, let's make a fucking film."

IN THE WOODS

CARLOS GUIDED **D**EAN back as Cody and Brad casually strolled down the trail. He was happy Cameron agreed to do the new lines. The dialogue wasn't stilted. It flowed more naturally, especially after they had their talks with Cody and Brad. He only hoped the sexual tension between the two transcribed into the film.

Cody's eyes were darting from Brad to the path. You could feel his nervousness. They came into the clearing that had been picked out. Brad stopped to take his shirt off. Cody's eyes lingered over his exposed skin. Absent-mindedly, Cody groped the hard outline of his cock through his shorts.

Smiling at Cody, Brad said, "It sure is nice out here."

"It sure is," Cody said, tearing his eyes off Brad and continuing on down the trail. He stopped suddenly and turned back to Brad. They collided. They grabbed on to each other to keep from falling over. Cody blurted out, "I'm sorry."

"It's okay." Brad looked down at Cody, the hint of a smile on his lips.

They stared into each other's eyes, neither wanting to let go. Brad leaned down. Cody stood on his tip toes. Carlos knew there were more lines, and was glad Cameron hadn't stopped the scene. Watching the two slowly move to share their first kiss was both beautiful and erotic. He wondered if it would be like that when he finally got to kiss Cameron.

It started with a tentative butterfly kiss on the lips, then their lips parted before they deepened it. Cody's hand moved up to the back of Brad's head and pulled him harder into the kiss. Brad pulled up Cody's tank top, revealing his rippling muscles. They broke the kiss long enough to toss the hindering garment away.

They were back on each other in an instant, transitioning from soft and hesitant to hungry and primal. Their bodies intertwined, pressing with need against one another, exploring. Hands roaming over territory only eyes once traveled and mouths gorging themselves with kisses on the once-forbidden skin.

Carlos would rewatch the scene in slow motion later to catch when Cody undid their shorts to let them fall down their muscular thighs; the movement was so quick. One minute their shorts were on, the next they were falling like magic to reveal twin eight-inch cocks jutting out from their matching trimmed bushes.

Cody guided Brad back to a fallen tree where Cody's shirt was tossed aside. Setting Brad down on the shirt, Cody moved between his spread legs, trapping their cocks between them. Precum dribbled over

their rubbing cocks as their intense kissing became ravenous.

Cody reached up behind Brad and fisted his hair. Pulling his head back, Cody licked and sucked up and down his exposed neck. Brad's eyes closed with a deep, rumbly groan. He had one hand on the back of Cody's head, the other steadying himself on the fallen tree trunk. Cody licked his way back up to Brad's lips.

"Jesus, Cody. You don't know how long I've wanted this," Brad moaned softly.

Cody paused. Running his gripping hand through Brad's floppy hair, Cody looked deep into his eyes. "As long as I have."

Their mouths collided once more. Cody began kissing his way down Brad's meaty chest until he found the strawberry-pink, quarter-sized nipples. Cody latched on causing Brad to release a deep, throaty moan. Cody ventured down, his hands drifting over Brad's body. Every touch of his lips on Brad was a promise to return.

Crouching down on the forest floor, Cody licked his way down past Brad's raging, hard cock. His mouth swaddled one of Brad's balls, then the other. Cody nudged Brad's legs wider, causing Brad to lean back and grip the fallen tree once again to steady himself. Cody ran his tongue over Brad's taint, and a euphoric delight spread across Brad's face.

"I want that ass," Cody said, pulling the larger man up, turning him around and bending him over the tree.

Spreading his legs wide and arching his back out, Brad's lust-filled voice proclaimed, "Take it! It's all ..." Brad finished the sentence with a groan, "fuck."

Cody buried his face between Brad's muscled melons. Carlos got great shots of Cody's tongue flicking and stroking Brad's tight pucker and also when Cody pulled back to brush his finger over the glistening hole. The look of unbridled passion and deep want on Cody's face as he enjoyed Brad was the best part.

Cameron was able to catch the identical expression on Brad's face as he whimpered and begged Cody to take him. The expression was raw and pure. It was the same expression Carlos saw reflected back in Cameron's eyes. The one they both would not act upon because they used the excuse of filming.

Cody licked down the length of Brad's cock. With his fingers plunging deep in Brad, Cody turned his body. He had his other arm slung around Brad's waist and his legs spread out wide. This gave everyone a spectacular view of the deep cut lines of his sculpted body as he nursed on Brad's dick.

Brad's hips rose and fell, fucking himself on Cody's probing fingers and fucking Cody's throat with his engorged cock. Brad's balls pelted Cody's chin as they bounced up and down. Carlos was about to stop them—as he was certain the bigger man was about to explode—but Brad acted first.

With Cody's mouth still savoring his cock and fingers exploring his ass, Brad stood up. Crouching down, he slipped his large hands under Cody's arms and lifted the compact man up into the air, pulling Cody out of his ass and off his cock. Brad sat him down delicately on the fallen tree.

Taking Cody's hands and pinning them behind his back, Brad worshiped Cody's body. His tongue traced over the hard lines of the defined muscles, flicked over the tiny, dime-sized nipples, and explored the ridges of Cody's well-defined abdominals. He traced his way down to Cody's balls.

Carefully and thoroughly bathing Cody's heavy balls in his mouth, Brad licked up the throbbing shaft to engulf Cody's crown. Swallowing him down and with his face nestled in Cody's groin, Brad forced himself to keep Cody buried in his throat. Pulling off to just the tip, he started bobbing up and down.

"Yeah, take that dick baby," Cody commanded, his voice deep and throaty. "Get it all nice and wet, it's going to be in your ass in a minute."

Brad pulled off Cody and looked needily up into his eyes. "I want you in me. I've wanted it for so long."

Cody broke free of Brad's grip and pushed him back onto the blanket Cameron surreptitiously placed there. "On your back."

Brad rolled onto his back. He brought his legs back into his chest, waiting for Cody, as Cody dropped down between Brad's legs. Sitting on his knees, Cody's eyes drank in the passive giant as he covertly lubed Brad and himself. One hand glided over his cock while the other slipped a lube-covered finger into Brad off-camera.

"You're so fucking sexy," Cody commented, placing his tip at Brad's entrance. Teasingly, he rubbed his cock over Brad's hole. "My beautiful Brad."

Cody pushed in slowly. Inch by inch, his cock disappeared with ease into Brad. He let out a sigh as he

sank all eight inches. There was no hint of pain on Brad's face, just the unmistakable look of pleasure and satisfaction of finally having Cody. The two joined looked more like lovers than they did actors.

Planting his muscular arms on either side of Brad, Cody's face hovered over Brad's. Brad, resting his legs on his shoulders, moved his hands to hold Cody close. They kissed, a deep soulful kiss Carlos envied. *He* wanted that. If not with Cameron, with someone who saw *him*, not who they wanted to see.

Cody's body rippled like a wave, his tight, muscly ass rising and falling. There was a slow roll of his hips, then another ripple, and then another. The ripples turned into waves that slowly built up turning into a tsunami repeatedly crashing softly into Brad. Each retreat was almost immediately met with the next crest of a wave.

The two shifted. Cody sat up on his knees. He twisted the bigger man easily so he lay on his side, one leg resting on Cody's shoulder, the other slipped under Cody. Brad let out a quiet wince when Cody's dick slipped from him, but an audible sigh of pleasure when Cody was sheathed in him once more.

Cody's hips moved like a roller coaster, twisting and turning at thrilling speeds. He held onto Brad's leg tightly while he pumped Brad's cock with his free hand. Brad moaned and begged for Cody to go faster, harder. Cody was all too willing to oblige, sliding his throbbing cock wildly into Brad.

Carlos was tempted to stop the action. From the intense look on Cody's face and the speed of his hip thrusts, he knew the precious money-shot was

imminent. They needed it on camera and not in Brad. They would have plenty of time to breed each other after, when they reshot portions of the scene, or alone in private.

Carlos's worry turned out to be unwarranted. Dropping Brad's leg, Cody pulled out and laid Brad flat on his back. With his cock pulsing and glistening in the filtered sun, Cody straddled Brad's waist and pumped his cock furiously. He had hunched over, one hand on Brad's chest, fingers digging into the hard flesh.

The sounds of a true orgasm escaped Cody's lips. "Oh, Brad," he panted over and over again. Cody released Brad's chest as he thrust his hips forward with the tossing of his head back. The culmination of their deed shot forth in white ribbons landing in sharp contrast across Brad's bronzed chest.

But, the moment wasn't over. Cody spent and still drunk on sex and lust, fell upon Brad. He pinned Brad's hands to the ground and kissed him tenderly. "Your turn," Cody announced, almost too quiet for them to catch. There was one more kiss, and then Cody was down between Brad's spread legs.

With Brad's cock in his mouth, Cody slipped two fingers back into Brad's ass, working his cock and ass at the same time. Cody pulled off and started stroking Brad just as the first blasts shot up in the air. Each blast rained down, landing all around them. Brad was crying out Cody's name while his body jerked about.

With Brad's cock spent, Cody moved to curl up next to Brad's exhausted body. Laying his head on

Brad's chest and playing with the drying rivers of cum, Cody sighed, "I can't believe we did that."

Brad's arm came around him and hugged him close. "I wish we had done it sooner."

Looking up at Brad, Cody smiled. "We'll have to make up for lost time."

The two kissed like long-time lovers. Carlos was lost in the moment watching them when Cameron yelled, "Cut!"

They waited a bit for the two to stop before they cleaned up and went over what needed to be reshot for the scene. Brad and Cody, their hands joined, covertly tossed glances at each other as they listened. Their cocks were quickly growing hard again at the prospect of playing naked with one another again.

18

BUG BITES, THORNS, AND A GUN

NATHAN'S EXHAUSTED, SLEEP-DEPRIVED body stumbled down the path. His skin burned from where the cruel underbrush whipped and cut into him from the few times he accidently strayed off the path during the night. He kept on, though, forcing one foot in front of the other, repeating to himself over and over, *I have to save them.*

Nathan saw the sky beginning to turn gray through patches in the trees. His mouth was dry with thirst, and he was almost tempted to bathe himself in the stagnant lake but remembered Daddy Walden's warning about the lake water making people violently ill.

Nathan stopped to rest for a moment against a tree. The camp was only a mile or so away. He could see it across the lake with his heavy eyes. With this path cleared, this trip was much quicker and easier than his first. He just wished he had the protective covering of clothes to help ward away the mosquitos leaving large welts on his skin.

I have to keep going, he told his addled brain. *Just a little farther and you can sleep all you want.*

Nathan remembered the first time he had walked this path. It was when Daddy Walden passed in his sleep. Nathan cried not knowing what to do. The pounding on the door startled him, and he had a glimmer of hope it was Ryan. Instead he found Corbin, screaming to be let in. He kept pounding on the door for over an hour before he left.

Nathan knew then he had to get help. He knew he had to get to Ryan at the camp. He couldn't trust anyone else. It had taken him a minute to gather his strength and determination. Slipping into some clothes, he went out the back door and to the path that Ryan used for his visits. That time had been easier with clothes and a bottle of water.

The sun was casting long shadows when he had finally got to the camp. He stayed in the woods looking for Ryan among the people who wandered through the camp. The sun was setting when Nathan finally spotted Ryan. He was so relieved that he just acted, bolting out of the woods, running as fast as he could toward Ryan. He kept his eyes focused solely on him as he cried out Ryan's name.

He slammed into Ryan full force, knocking both of them to the ground. The words came spilling out of Nathan like water out of a broken pitcher. Ryan somehow made sense of his manic gibberish and calmed him down. He quickly took charge. He told Nathan to wait for him in the woods.

"I'm going to call for help from the office, and then I'm coming back for you," he remembered Ryan explaining.

It seemed like forever before Ryan came back on his four-wheeler. Pulling Nathan up behind him, they sped off down the trail. Nathan clutched Ryan tightly, grateful for Ryan rescuing him yet again.

When the ambulance came, Ryan handled everything for Nathan. When Corbin came back trying to get in the house, Ryan had gone out and run the man off. Ryan had stayed and helped him deal with Daddy Walden's passing. He wouldn't admit it, but Ryan had no idea what was going to happen to Nathan.

Then, Daddy Lin showed up. They had both been suspicious about Daddy Lin until the cute, little, muscly man, Cody, came and told them about Daddy Lin running Corbin off the property. They were also able to confirm the emails from Daddy Walden asking him to come work at the camp.

It had taken time, but Nathan grew comfortable with Daddy Lin. Ryan helped, but Nathan couldn't take his eyes off the sexy man. After a few months, Ryan stayed back at the camp, and he was alone with Daddy Lin. That time alone together was all that was needed to kindle the fire of their love.

Nathan pushed off the tree and trudged down the path again. He went on a few steps before stopping again. The sounds of the night faded away with the rising of the sun. That's what allowed Nathan to hear the violent crushing of footsteps behind him seasoned heavily with the angry voices of two men.

"Corbin and Rafi," Nathan mouthed their names with terror.

A knot formed in the pit of his stomach. He couldn't be caught, not now. He had to hide, but he didn't know where. He looked to the poisonous lake, then to the ruthless forest. He took his chances with the abusive forest. If they did find him in the thickets, at least they'd come out just as scratched up as him.

Carefully slipping behind a tree, Nathan heard the heated voices coming closer. Quelling his fear, he pushed his way into the foliage. Thorns drew blood as they scratched his skin. Nathan held in the cries of pain. Tiny trickles of blood formed on his skin where the sharp barbs dug.

From behind the cover of the villainous plants, Nathan saw the two men step into view. They huffed with anger and the exertion of rushing after him. Nathan had a short-lived worry they'd find him when they paused near his hiding spot. Then, he worried about Daddy Lin and his friends trapped back in the playroom.

"I can't believe you let him escape!" Rafi growled furiously.

Corbin, trying to catch his breath, returned, "I didn't let him escape! I don't know how he got out of that cage."

"Why the fuck did I let you talk me into this?" Rafi asked, crowding Corbin. "There's no money!"

Corbin tried to push back, but his thin body just bounced off Rafi. "There is money! I know there is!"

"What I know," Nathan heard the metal cocking of a gun, "is that I'm tired of this bullshit."

"Rafi, please, don't." Hearing the genuine fear in Corbin's voice, Nathan covered his mouth with his hands. "You need me to find the money."

Nathan saw Rafi's arm was raised. He caught the glint of the metal. "There is no fucking money. We would have found it by now. We destroyed that house looking for it."

"There is! I'm telling you there is! We just have to get them to talk!" Corbin pleaded, slowly backing away.

Rafi menacingly stepped toward Corbin. "That's the other thing. Now I have to figure out what to do with all the bodies. I can't just let them go."

"We'll set the place on fire!" Corbin blurted out. "We'll blame it on the kid. We'll make him write a note taking credit for it all."

Rafi had the gun pressed to Corbin's forehead now. "One problem. We don't have the kid."

"I'll find him! I swear!" Corbin was panicking now. "He must be hiding out near the house. We would have found him by now if he came this way."

Nathan closed his eyes and held his hand over his mouth to keep from screaming. The explosion from the gun echoed in the woods. When he opened them, he expected to see Corbin's lifeless body crumpled on the ground, but Rafi had held the gun straight up in the air at the last minute, shooting the gun as a scare tactic.

"We better find him, or it's *you* who's writing the note," Rafi warned, shoving Corbin down the trail.

They headed down the trail, away from the camp and away from Nathan. He could hear Corbin

frantically saying to Rafi, "We'll find that little brat. I promise."

When the voices faded away and the sound of their crunching footsteps vanished in the distance, Nathan carefully inched his way out of the under-brush. More scratches and cuts began to litter his mosquito-feasted body. His head still swam with its need to sleep, and his body cried out for rest. Nathan ignored them both; he had to press on. He had to get to the camp, get to Ryan. Ryan would know what to do. He would help Nathan rescue Daddy Lin and his friends. Then, he could sleep.

Putting one step in front of the other, Nathan pushed on. *I have to do this.*

19

A FUCKING SHOWER SCENE

THEY HAD GREAT shots of Mitch tromping through the woods into the communal shower. Now Dean and Mitch were doing some last-minute rehearsing while everyone else was setting up inside. That is, when they weren't pulling Brad and Cody off each other. Cameron couldn't blame them. He could barely keep his hands off Carlos.

"Enough!" Ryan cried out, pulling Cody from Brad's embrace. "I know you boys just discovered the joys of sex, but we have work to do." Ryan pushed a laughing Cody to the other side of the room. "*You* stay on this side of the room," he glared over at an amused Brad, "and *you* stay on that side." Turning his head back and forth to scowl at them both, he warned, "If I even catch a meaningful glance between you two, there will be hell to pay."

They returned to their duties only to be startled at the yelps of dismay coming from Brad and Cody. Their arms covered their faces at the blasts of two small water pistols Ryan was rapidly unloading at them.

"I said not even a meaningful glance," Ryan scolded, lowering his toy weapons.

Wiping his face, Cody foolishly said, "It wasn't meaningful, it was flirting." A squirt of water hit him in the left eye. "Hey!"

Brad made to tend to Cody, but Ryan held him at bay with the other water gun. "Go ahead. I've always wanted to unload all over your pretty face."

Brad gawked. Cameron and Carlos erupted into uncontrollable laughter that spread to Mitch and Dean, then to Cody and Brad. Ryan tried to keep a straight face, but eventually his face cracked. Lowering his weapons, he doubled over in laughter.

"I swear, I meant that to sound threatening," Ryan laughed.

Cameron, trying to regain some composure, wiped the tears from his eyes. "Okay guys, let's get into places."

"I have a question," Dean spoke up, raising his hand like he was in school.

Cameron groaned internally. "What?"

"Why is Mitch fucking me, instead of me fucking Mitch?" Dean asked. "I've got the bigger dick."

"Because we don't have twelve hours for you to jam all of your pant python into me," Mitch chirped merrily.

"It's not *that* big," Dean groaned.

The room went silent, then everyone simultaneously said, "Yes, it is."

Mitch put a consoling hand on Dean's shoulder. "We can flip fuck, but I fuck you first."

"Fine, but I get to eat your ass," Dean countered.

Mitch huffed. "Okay, but when you blow your load on my face, you better get me a wash cloth after."

"I always do," Dean argued. "You're the one that never wants to sit on my face."

"That's because your tongue goes almost as deep as your dick," Mitch playfully nudged back.

Cameron inched over to Ryan. In a low voice he asked, "What are we watching? Are they …"

"Flirting? Yes," Ryan groaned.

The two kept on, verbally sparring. Cameron turned back to Ryan. "Is that …"

"How Carlos and you act?" Ryan gave him a side eye. "Yes."

"To be fair—"

"You two just need to fuck," Ryan cut him off.

"I second that." Cameron startled at Carlos's sudden appearance at his side. "Are you sure we can't film my stuff today, too?"

Cameron ignored him. "Guys! Guys! Can we use this energy in the scene? Brad! Cody! Quit making out!" Cameron jumped at the casual hand-petting of his ass. He glared at Carlos. "Get your hand off my ass."

"But, Chipmunk, it's cute and you're supposed to pet cute things." Carlos squeezed his ass before withdrawing his hand.

"Stop calling me Chipmunk, Latin Lover," Cameron growled, his voice more playful than bite.

Cameron jumped with the playful swat of Carlos's hand on his bottom. "Yes, sir, Chipmunk." Grinning,

Carlos winked at him then turned his attention to Dean and Mitch. "Guys, we talked about this. Dean, you're not fucking Mitch this scene because I'm fucking him next and after you, it'll be like throwing a hotdog down a hallway."

"It already is," Ryan piped in.

"Hey!" Mitch shot Ryan a dirty look.

"Everyone!" Cameron bellowed, tired of the antics. "How about we let you two just do what comes natural?"

Dean and Mitch looked at each other with mischievous smiles and said, "Okay."

"Stay on script with the lines," Carlos warned. "You can ad lib the sex but keep it sensual. Have fun with it. Pretend you actually want to have sex with each other." Carlos paused at a snort of laughter from Ryan. "Just have fun."

"Oh, no! Never tell these two deviants that." Ryan stepped forward to stand beside Carlos. "Boys, I want you to see who can make the other moan the loudest." Cheshire grins spread on both men's faces. "Are we ready?"

"I'm so going to win," Mitch said with an impish tone.

Dean jeered back, "Want to bet?"

"Guys, how about showing us instead of telling us?" Cameron spoke up. "Let's get this scene shot. Mitch, get in place. Dean, lose the shorts and start the shower." Cameron didn't mean to gawk when Dean's shorts hit the floor. "Jesus."

"What?" Dean asked, grabbing his cock by the base and twirling his twelve-inch, semi-hard beef stick. "Okay, it is that big."

"Jealous that his is that big, or that Mitch can take it?" Carlos whispered in his ear.

Cameron swallowed hard. "How can he take all that?"

"Practice," Mitch answered proudly, walking past them.

"The human anus can stretch up to seven inches before taking damage, and raccoons can squeeze into holes as tight as four inches," Carlos spoke matter-of-factly. "That means he can fit almost two raccoons up his ass, so taking Dean isn't that big of a deal."

Cameron turned his head and gaped at Carlos. "What?"

"It's a fact. Look it up." Carlos shrugged, walking over to Cody to help line up the shots.

Cameron reached for his phone, but then remembered he left it back at the cabin since it had no signal. "Can we focus already? We have a fucking shower scene to film."

There were some soft giggles as everyone took their places and Dean started the shower. Cameron took up position behind Brad and lined up the camera. He looked over at Carlos who was doing the same with Cody. Ryan had the sound equipment and gave him a thumbs up.

Cameron pointed to Dean. He got under the spray and pretended to soap himself up. He looked at Mitch, who gave him a nod. Focusing back at Dean casually rubbing his hands over his body as the water sprayed down on him, Cameron said, "Action."

Both cameras started recording.

Cameron watched Dean go from casual soaping to running his hands over his defined slightly hairy chest, to down over his firm stomach. Just as he was about to reach his cock, he turned around to show his perfectly rounded ass. When he turned again, cock swinging like a pendulum, he casually stroked himself as the water trickled down his body.

Dean turned and Mitch walked into the shot. "Mind if I join you?" Mitch asked, the words striking Cameron with familiarity.

Mitch didn't wait for an answer. He stripped out of his clothes and joined Dean under the spray. Their bodies were pressed close together, mouths almost touching. Mitch's hard seven-or-so inches were pressed into Dean's thigh. Dean had his hand on the small of Mitch's back. They were a hair's breadth from kissing.

"I'm done in the shower." The words Dean spoke low and seductive now were the same Cameron remembered saying the day before.

Mitch's hand pushed the wet hair from Dean's face. "Wash my back first?"

Mitch leaned in for a kiss. Cameron expected Dean to turn away and the very same thing he said to come from Dean's lips. He, instead, met Mitch's lips with his. Cameron expected something rough and sloppy, but what he got was something carnal, yet soft.

Dean held Mitch in his arms. Mitch had one hand running his hands through Dean's wet hair, the other clutching Dean's back. With the water cascading over their bodies, Cameron would have thought them two lovers rather than verbally fencing buddies.

Dean made the first move, kissing down the length of Mitch's neck. He left a trail of kisses on a familiar path down Mitch's body. The water stopped. Mitch had both hands in Dean's wet hair. Cameron could see the words forming on Mitch's trembling lips.

"Oh, baby, yeah," Mitch moaned at Dean's flicking tongue at the tip of his cock. "Come on. Suck me. I missed that mouth on my cock." Dean's impossibly long tongue curled around Mitch's cock. "Come on, don't tease. Please."

Cameron thought he heard a slight chuckle of triumph before Dean retracted his tongue and spread his lips over the crown of Mitch's dick. Unable to control his need to have Dean swallow him, Mitch thrusted his hips forwards. He held a willing Dean in his groin for a brief moment before he started face-fucking him.

Dean gripped Mitch's hip, helping pull the man into his mouth. His other hand started stroking the impossibly large slab of meat between his legs. Cameron was distracted by the twelve inches of flesh rapidly inflating before his eyes. Mitch was not. He was steadily pumping his cock into Dean's mouth.

Cameron watched, remembering how he lay in bed while Carlos teased and toyed with his body.

Dean pulled off of Mitch, and after doing what can only be described as impressive sexual acrobatics, Dean was on his back on the wet tile floor with Mitch straddling his face. Dean was tongue-fucking Mitch's ass. Mitch was choking down eight of Dean's inches.

Cameron motioned Carlos to get a close-up of Mitch devouring Dean's cock; he now had almost all of the gargantuan cock down his gullet. At the

same time, Cameron had Brad move in on Dean eating Mitch out. The man's tongue was whipping wildly about in flicks and lashes before darting in and snaking into Mitch.

It wasn't long before Mitch surprised Dean by pulling off his dick and mouth. Dean twisted with Mitch's strong hands to his stomach then got up on all fours. "Oh, baby. We can't go this long without fucking again." With a hand on the small of Dean's back he pushed his cock in. Mitch let out a sigh, "It feels just like I remember."

"I missed this, too," Dean moaned, arching his back. "We've got to stop sneaking around."

Mitch playfully slapped Dean's ass. "Says who?" Mitch started rocking his hips into Dean. "Sneaking around is half the fun. Fuck, you feel so good." Mitch grabbed Dean's hips. "I just want to be able to kiss you in front of the others."

"Me, too." Dean was meeting each of Mitch's thrusts. "Let's tell them."

Mitch pulled out and flipped Dean onto his back like a pancake. "Let's tell the world." Mitch straddled Dean. To everyone's amazement, Mitch slowly lowered himself onto Dean without a trace of pain or hesitation.

"Oh, baby," Dean groaned, one hand on Mitch's hip to help steady him, the other exploring his chest. "Damn, you're just as tight as ever."

If Mitch had wanted to say anything, he couldn't. With all of Dean in him, he was doing breathing exercises. He took the hand Dean used exploring his chest

in his own. He brought it to his lips to kiss the back of Dean's hand, then rode the man like a bucking bronco.

Cameron hated that he couldn't get a better view of Mitch taking Dean. Using Dean's hand for support, Mitch was rocketing up and crashing down on Dean's hips. Amazingly enough, he was stroking his own cock with the same fervor. Both men were moaning and groaning with the pleasure they were giving each other.

"Oh, baby," Mitch grimaced, "I can't hold it back anymore."

Dean tightened his grip on Mitch. "All over my face, baby. Paint me with your cum."

It was then Cameron realized nothing they said since the sex started was scripted. He was brought back to the moment with a guttural groan from Mitch. With Dean's help, he slipped up along Dean's body and fell forward, planting one hand on the slick tile floor, while his other hand continued beating his meat.

Cameron nudged Brad to zoom in on his cock. Wordlessly he directed Carlos to move around to get a front-view angle. The moment came with a roar, followed by a whimper. White sticky love shot out of Mitch, covering Dean's face and splattering across the tiled shower floor.

Mitch's body trembled and shook with the exertion. Dean grabbed him by the chest and they exchanged places. With cum dripping down his face, Dean stood over Mitch. Gathering the cum from his face, he used both hands to stroke himself. Mitch smiled blissfully under him, his hand running up and down Dean's legs.

"Come on, baby. Give me that load," Mitch purred from below. "Empty those balls all over me."

It took a few minutes, but Dean's cock exploded. An impressive load gushed forth, bathing Mitch down below. Cameron wasn't sure if Dean was ever going to stop. When the last bit dribbled out, Dean's legs buckled and he fell on top of Mitch. They held each other, faces dripping with their sex and they kissed.

Cameron watched, a little turned on and a little stunned. It took him a moment to finally say, "Cut."

"Holy fuck, I can't believe he took all that," Carlos blurted out.

Ryan stepped forward with two washcloths. "So, you two are officially an item now?"

"Yeah," Mitch laughed. "I guess we are."

Ryan dropped the warm cloth on Mitch's face. "About damn time."

"I think we're done for a while," Cameron announced, adjusting his hard-on.

Walking past Cameron, Ryan winked. "I think Carlos can help you with that. I'm going to get some fresh air. This place reeks of sex."

"Too bad my scene isn't until tomorrow. Otherwise …" Carlos teased.

Cameron thought for a second. "You know, we could change up who has the solo scene."

"Yeah?" Carlos smiled at him.

Brad chimed in, "Cody and I need to find out what's wrong with the phone line."

"We need an actual shower now," Dean laughed, snuggling Mitch.

Cameron mulled it over for a moment. "I can shoot it alone. I can use tripods."

"Sounds good to me." Carlos winked at Cameron. "Am I using toys?"

Cameron was about to answer when Ryan came back in, visibly agitated. "I heard a gunshot. I'm going to take one of the four-wheelers and check on Lin and Nathan. Cody, Brad. I want you to get that phone up and working."

"What do you want us to do?' Mitch asked, untangling himself from Dean.

"What's the big deal?" Cameron asked, confused. "It's probably just hunters."

"There's no hunting here, and the only roads into these woods are to this camp and Nathan's house," Ryan answered.

"Do you want one of us to come with you?" Carlos slipped a protective hand around Cameron's waist.

"No, I'll take one of the radios with me. If there's a problem I'll radio back for you guys to get the police." Ryan looked at the worried faces. "It might be nothing."

"Be careful." Cameron put a comforting hand on Ryan's shoulder.

STROKE THAT BIG DICK FOR ME

"**A**RE YOU SURE we should be filming?" Carlos asked from the bed. He was lying down on his back as Cameron moved around adjusting the cameras and lighting for his impromptu solo scene. "Shouldn't we be, you know, doing something?"

"We are doing something," Cameron answered, looking at Carlos from behind the lens of a camera. "We're filming. What else can we do? Cody and Brad are fixing the phone line. Ryan went to check on Lin and Nathan. Brad and Dean are making lunch and waiting for Ryan to radio back. What else do you want us to do?"

Carlos gave Cameron a salacious look. "We could make out."

"I don't kiss." Cameron stepped out from behind the camera. "Okay, start out on your stomach, then roll over, and pretend to wake up."

Carlos pulled off his shirt to reveal his long lean body. "Are you going to help me prep my tool?"

Carlos shucked his shorts, and his ten-inch hard dick flopped about.

"From what I can see, you don't need help, Latin Lover." Cameron let out a sound of annoyance. "Why aren't you wearing underwear?"

Carlos reached over into a small bag he retrieved from their cabin and responded, "Chipmunk, chill." He held up a black jockstrap and a pair of white briefs. "We weren't supposed to film, remember? Which one?"

Carlos watched Cameron's eyes dart between the two. He didn't need to look at the tent in Cameron's pants to know he was getting turned on. "The white. It'll look better against your skin."

"But, the jock frames my ass." Carlos dropped the jock back into the bag before shimmying into the briefs. He adjusted himself in the briefs. "How do I look, Chipmunk?" Carlos asked, massaging himself through the thin fabric.

Carlos watched Cameron switch into professional mode, visibly suppressing his animalistic desire. "Stop fucking around." Carlos moved his hand from his cock. "The white is sexier. Now, lay on your stomach. You're going to pretend to wake up."

"Like this?" Carlos flipped over. He put his hand under his head and slightly pushed up to stick his butt out. Cameron smacked his ass. "Oh, Daddy."

"Look natural, not like you're humping the pillows." Carlos felt Cameron's hands on him, moving his legs and adjusting his underwear. "I know it's porn, but I want it to be decent."

"Yes, sir, Mr. Chipmunk, sir," Carlos teased, letting Cameron position his body on the bed.

Cameron stood back to admire his work. "Perfect." He pointed a finger at Carlos. "No comments." Carlos's comment died on his tongue. "Okay, I'm going to get footage of you on your stomach pretending to sleep, then we'll have you wake up. You'll roll over and start running your hand over your body. Next, you'll start playing with your dick."

"Anything in particular?" Carlos asked, stepping back into professional mode. "And what about my hole? Should I use toys?"

Cameron thought about it. "No toys. I think it'll be hotter if you finger yourself. If I'm wrong, we'll film that later. What I really want you to do is go with it. Put on a show for someone who isn't watching."

"Got it," Carlos said after a moment of thought. He was going to put on a show, alright. Closing his eyes, he said, "Ready?" Carlos gave him a slight nod. "Action. Stroke that big dick for me."

Carlos heard Cameron moving to let the camera capture his youthful body. He evened out his breathing, taking long deep breaths and letting them out to give the illusion of sleep. In his mind, he wasn't performing on camera for some stranger. He wasn't performing at all.

In Carlos's mind, he was just waking up and missing Cameron. That would be the reason for his morning excitement. The idea of the two of them together was the reason for his current excitement. He knew it was foolish to think after knowing each other for a little less than twenty-four hours they'd be lifetime lovers. That only happened in books and movies.

Carlos wanted to see where this thing between him and Cameron went. He didn't want to be like Dennis, too scared to love. He didn't want to be like Hunter and Mark, realizing they lost the best thing they ever had, only to be lucky enough to find it years later. Then, there was Billy who could have lost his chance at love because he didn't realize he was in a relationship.

"Carlos." Cameron calling his name brought him out of his little fantasy. "Roll over."

Carlos did an exaggerated stretch and shifted his body as he rolled over. Neither of them said anything while Cameron moved the camera up and down his slender toned body. Carlos counted to thirty, then started running his hands over his chest and stomach. He fluttered his eyes open and gave a salacious smile.

He saw Cameron was catching it all. Carlos moved his hands down to fondle himself. Cameron was trying to be professional, but Carlos could see the interest in his face from behind the camera. Catching Cameron's eye, Carlos decided this wasn't going to be a show for someone who wasn't watching. He was going to give the best damn show for someone who was.

Carlos looked through the camera at Cameron. He ran his hand along the outline of his length while he humped up into his hand. He ran the tip of his tongue over his slightly parted lips. He brought his finger to his mouth and sucked on it before lowering it to play with his tiny brown nipple.

The hand rubbing his cock moved to dip under the waistband of his briefs. Carlos rolled his balls in his hand. Biting his lower lip, Carlos continued humping

the air. A wet spot of precum slowly grew at the tip of his dick. Jerking on camera was different this time. He felt it, deep in his belly, this desire to perform. Not for the camera, but for Cameron.

Carlos felt the heat of passion rising in him. His cock vibrated with the need to be touched. Pulling his hand from his briefs, he slipped his other hand down from his nipple. He ran his hands over his groin, making soft whimpers. He needed to touch himself, and he needed to be touched.

Raising his hips, Carlos slipped the briefs down over his butt, then over his hard cock. Slipping them down his legs, he tossed them aside. He laid with his legs spread wide. Free now, his cock jerked and twitched about. Carlos ran a finger over the head of his cock, covering it in precum. He stared directly through the camera at Cameron while he tasted himself.

He pulled a small bottle of lube out. He held his hard, ten inches straight up in the air. Holding the bottle over his cock, he drizzled cool lube from the bottle. He ran the hand holding his cock up and down to coat it, making it shiny and wet. Setting the bottle down, he reached down between his spread legs and rubbed the outside of his hole.

Carlos kept his eyes focused on Cameron. He could see his own lust and desire mirrored back at him. He pretended this wasn't just a jerk-off video. He was on a video call with Cameron, and they were sharing a long distance moment together. Cameron would be on the other side of the screen, playing with his hole and jerking his own cock as they said dirty nasty things to each other.

Carlos took his time, moving his hand at a steady, slow place up and down his shaft, the head of his cock popping out of the foreskin. He moved his hand slowly over his cock, feeling the hard vein running across the top of his shaft, the bump half way up, and the silky feel of his skin. He had edged himself before, and hated it. With Cameron's eyes on him, he never wanted to shoot.

With the palm of his hand, Carlos pushed his cock toward the camera and held it there for a moment. A droplet of precum formed on his tip, then dropped down leaving a sticky trail in the air. He let go, allowing his cock to swing back and thump his hard toned belly. He took his cock in hand again and, with his cock pointed at his face, resumed his slow and languid stroking.

Carlos chewed on his lower lip. His hips started raising up, pushing his cock through his clenched fist. He wanted to climax so badly, wanted to shoot his load all over himself while Cameron watched. Carlos wanted him to see how he made him climax without even touching him, but he also wanted Cameron to never take his arms off him.

Carlos flipped over. With his knees on the bed he arched his back to put his ass on full display. His face pressed into the mattress while he pushed his dripping cock back between his legs and slowly ran a wet finger over his hairless hole. He pushed a single finger in, then a second. He started to fuck himself on his wiggling fingers.

He groaned low and deep, thinking of Cameron doing a similar show for him. He remembered the

sexy sweet sounds Cameron made for him the day before. They were soft and deprived. They were the sounds of someone who hadn't had his needs properly cared for in a long time.

Carlos couldn't contain himself any longer. Pulling his fingers from his hole, he flipped again. He took his cock with one hand and his balls with the other. He pumped his cock furiously with his eyes fixated on Cameron. There was no stopping him now. He was about to shoot the biggest load of his life.

Closing his eyes and gritting his teeth, Carlos arched his back up. His hips bucked up and he tossed his head back and forth. His hole clenched. His balls tingled. He snarled right before his cock started pulsing and launched the milky white seed all over his body.

His body tensed with the jolting orgasm that resonated in his body. Shock wave after shock wave surged through him until the quakes turned into minor tremors. He exhaled with a satiated sigh. He beamed a satisfied gluttonous smile at Cameron while he milked the last bit of bliss from his cock.

Letting go of his cock and balls, he ran his hands over his body, rubbing in the cum. He pretended it was Cameron's and that it was Cameron running his hand over his body. He wanted nothing more at that moment than to take Cameron in his arms and kiss the young man until their lips hurt.

"Cut," Cameron said, voice hot and bothered. "Wow, I didn't expect that. That was amazing." He grabbed the wipes and a towel for Carlos. "It felt like you were doing the show just for me."

I was, Carlos wanted to say, taking the wipes from Cameron.

"I'm glad you didn't use the toys." Cameron took a wipe and began wiping the drying cum off Carlos's stomach.

Carlos's hand grabbed his. Cameron looked at him perplexed. "You should go now," Carlos said, a bit of hurt in his voice. "If you don't I'm going to pull you into this bed and kiss you."

"Okay." Cameron pulled his hand back from Carlos.

There was a bit of bitterness in Carlos's voice when he said, "You don't kiss. Remember?"

"Right," Cameron nodded. "I'll wait outside, okay?"

Carlos saw the hesitation in Cameron. He moved with uncertain steps out of the room, looking back from the door and smiling a halfhearted smile at Carlos. He didn't say anything before shutting the door behind him, leaving Carlos there in his own sticky mess.

21

I DID IT ONCE

NATHAN PUSHED HIS body on. The adrenaline burst he had earlier faded and left him as exhausted and foggy-brained as before, if not more. He couldn't stop, though. He wouldn't stop. No matter how much his body cried out in pain or for rest, he'd push on. He had to.

Daddy Lin needed him to make it. Daddy Lin's friends needed him to make it and he needed to get to Ryan. If he didn't, there was no telling what would happen. He couldn't run away, like he did from that cruel man who brought him to the camp. He loved Daddy Lin and needed to protect Daddy Lin like Daddy Lin protected him.

It didn't matter his body was covered in bleeding bug bites, scabbed over cuts that tore open, or that his feet were blistered and cut raw. He had walked this path before, when Daddy Walden passed away in his sleep. He pushed through his pain and fear that day, and he could do it now.

Ryan was good to his word then, talking to the police and the paramedics when they came. He stayed with Ryan that night, and the next morning when Corbin came back, Ryan had run him off. They were lucky when Daddy Lin showed up the next day, though they hadn't trusted him until he had proven who he was.

Ryan didn't trust Daddy Lin until Brad and Cody were able to hack into Daddy Walden's email and confirm the story. Even then, he was hesitant to trust Daddy Lin. He was staying at the camp that weekend to see what he was getting into, to see what he was taking over.

Nathan had slowly grown comfortable with Daddy Lin, mainly because Nathan found him so attractive. It had been a long and slow process until one night, he crept into Daddy Lin's bed and curled up next to him. That was the beginning of their odd sort of courtship. Daddy Lin fought it, but in the end the two damaged men found their hearts intertwined.

That's why Nathan was pushing through the forest now, struggling to put one foot in front of the other, letting insects use him as an all-you-can-eat buffet, while plants tore apart his skin. He loved Daddy Lin. He had to do whatever it took to save him. Daddy Lin would and had already done it for Nathan.

"Keep going," Nathan told himself softly. His lips were dry and cracking. He swayed with each excruciating step. He thought he saw something coming toward him from the camp. Then, he noticed the buzz of an engine. Nathan smiled. He knew who it was, without a doubt.

Nathan wanted to run to meet him, but it was taking everything he had to just stand there watching Ryan on his four-wheeler get closer. He waved weakly at Ryan, who slowed to a stop and bounded off his ride, rushing to Nathan. He caught Nathan right when his body began crumbling to the ground.

"Nathan, what happened?" he heard Ryan's panicked voice ask. "Where's Lin?"

Nathan blinked. This was a dream. It had to be. Nathan let out a dry raspy laugh. "You know. Corbin and that other man have him locked up with his buddies." Nathan reached up and touched Ryan's face. "I escaped though. Sshh. Don't tell anyone."

Nathan felt himself being lifted up. "I'm taking you back to the camp."

"You always rescue me," Nathan said, the deliriousness of exhaustion firmly taking hold of him. "I don't deserve a friend like you."

Ryan set him down on the seat of the four-wheeler. "Save your strength. I need you to hold on tight to me." Nathan reached out to touch Ryan's face. Ryan stopped him from falling over. "Stay with me." Ryan slipped in front of him. "Hey guys, this is Ryan. Do you hear me?"

Nathan laughed. "Yes, I hear you."

"It's Dean. Go." Came a voice out of the air. Nathan looked around to see who else was there.

Nathan heard a strange static in the air then Ryan speaking to someone who wasn't there. "We need an ambulance to the camp and police to the house. Corbin's back and this time he brought a friend."

I NEED TO GET MY SHIT TOGETHER

CAMERON TURNED AND looked at the door he just closed hoping Carlos would yank it open and take him in his arms. How had he let this sexy goof sneak into his heart? Especially after finding out he was friends with not just one, but two people involved in the ending of his engagement. How would his sexy Latin lover react if he knew he was Alex's ex-fiancé?

Turning away from the door and leaving the Barracks, Cameron decided there was only one thing he could do: seek advice. With Ryan checking on Lin and Nathan, that meant there was only one person from whom he could get trusted advice, his Aunt Lexi on the other side of the country.

What am I doing? he asked himself, kicking at the ground as he made his way back to the cabin. *I shouldn't be getting involved with someone else who films porn.*

Cameron stopped when he saw Dean on his four-wheeler zooming toward him, dust and rock flinging behind as he passed Cameron. Cameron shrugged and moved on, not thinking anything of it. He needed to talk to his Aunt Lexi. She would help him get his shit together.

What am I doing here? What do I think I'm doing? That scene I just filmed was cruel for the both of us. I can't let Carlos think there's going to be something more after all this is over. He lives across the country.

Cameron turned down the path to the cabin. He knew he had to come clean with Carlos. He had to tell him flat out that once this shoot was over, they were over. He just wasn't sure about telling him about Alex, or his strange connections with Billy and Dennis. That might encourage Carlos. He needed to talk to Lexi.

Grabbing his phone and keys from the cabin, Cameron got into his piece of shit rental and headed out of the campgrounds. Passing the Barracks, he saw Carlos standing out front, probably looking for him.

He couldn't stop, even though he wanted to. Talking to Carlos right now would muddle everything. He'd look into Carlos's smiling, brown eyes and do the one thing he shouldn't: kiss him.

Out onto the main road, Cameron's phone exploded with notifications when the life energy of service flowed back into it. Fighting the urge to check his phone, Cameron first slowed down before pulling off the road onto the grassy shoulder.

Slamming the rented clunker into park, Cameron grabbed his phone littered with notifications. He quickly cleared away the ones he didn't really care about, allowing him to see the dozens of texts his Aunt Lexi sent, each one more urgent than the last

based on the amount of exclamation points. He didn't bother to read the messages before he called.

"It's about time you called me!" Lexi answered angrily. "I've been texting and calling you all day!"

"There's no service at the camp, remember?" Cameron responded immediately. "What's going on?"

Cameron heard her make a sound of annoyance before she continued. "Anyways, I talked to Josh's husband right after we talked this morning. He said Josh called him right before they lost service, and he hasn't heard from him since."

"But they didn't show up at the camp," Cameron responded.

Lexi let out a sound of annoyance. "Cameron, how hard is your head hitting that headboard?" He was taken back by the question. "They should be there. They were supposed to visit Lin Max, then head over to the camp. I need you to head over Lin Max's and see if they are okay."

"Gunshot," Cameron said, remembering Ryan's worry from earlier.

That sent Lexi into a panic. "What? You heard a gunshot?"

Cameron shook his head before remembering Lexi couldn't see him. "No, Ryan did. Earlier. He went to—" Dread filled Cameron. Ryan had gone to the house. "Aunt Lexi, I got to go."

Cameron hung the phone up. Tossing it on the seat beside him, he put the SUV in gear and slammed on the gas, sending dirt and grass showering behind him. Turning the vehicle roughly around in the road, he ignored the sound of his Aunt Lexi repeatedly calling him back.

Fuck! Fuck! Fuck! How could I be so fucking self-absorbed? Cameron took a hard right back down the road to the camp. Loose gravel and dirt shot out from under his speeding wheels. In the distance he could see something coming toward him. He squinted to see Brad on one of the four-wheelers coming toward him.

He didn't slow down and neither did Cameron. They sped past each other. Cameron pushed the SUV harder, fearing someone was hurt. Passing the office, he saw two more four-wheelers coming toward him. He slowed down. He watched them pull off to the Barracks.

23

WHAT DID I DO?

CARLOS LOOKED AT the door Cameron just closed between them. He felt guilty for running Cameron off. He hadn't meant the words he said to come out so bitterly, only to be a warning. The words were right, they just came out wrong. Or maybe they came out right.

Carlos wiped off the rest of his spunk, then slipped into his shorts and shoes. At any rate, he needed to go talk to Cameron. They needed to clear the air between them. They had scenes to shoot. They were sharing a cabin. Hell, they were sharing a bed. If he needed to, he'd sleep on the couch in the cabin or in the Barracks with the rest of the guys. He just had to find Cameron first to make sure everything was okay.

Stepping out of the room, Carlos called out, "Cameron!" When no reply came, Carlos looked in every room before stepping outside. "Cameron!" He called again. *He must have gone back to the cabin.* Carlos took the path out to the road.

138

"What the hell?" Carlos watched Cameron speed past him. "Where the hell is he going?"

He was leaving. Carlos knew it. He scared Cameron off. It wasn't like Cameron had anything to pack. The airport still hadn't found his luggage. He could board a plane and be gone. He didn't owe anyone here any obligations.

"Hey, Carlos!" Dean called over the roar of his four-wheeler. He slowed to a stop. "Where's Cameron going? We need his SUV."

Carlos shrugged. "I … I don't know. I think he left. What's going on?"

"Cody, fill him in. I got to get back to the Cantina," Dean ordered.

Cody barely hopped off the back before Dean tore off like a bat out of Hell. With a camp radio in one hand, Cody grabbed Carlos's hand with the other and pulled him back into the Barracks. "Whoever cut the phone lines also sliced the tires on our van and your truck."

"Hunter is going to kill me," Carlos groaned.

Cody continued, ignoring the comment. Letting go of Carlos's hand he rushed into their tiny kitchen. "Brad is going to the main road to call the police and an ambulance."

"Stop for a minute." Carlos grabbed the squat man by the shoulders when he rushed by. "Cody, what's going on?"

Cody took a deep breath and let it all out at once as he spoke rapidly. "Ryan found Nathan on the trail, all cut up and covered in bug bites. He said something about Corbin and a friend being at Lin's house.

Ryan is bringing Nathan back here, but we can't call for help at the office because the phone lines are cut, and we can't go for help or take Nathan to the hospital because our tires are slashed, and Cameron just left with the only working vehicle and that gunshot Ryan heard—"

Carlos put a hand over Cody's mouth to get him to stop. "You do realize I don't understand a single thing you're talking about other than the phone lines are cut, our tires are slashed, and someone needs help." Cody nodded. "Are we in danger?" Cody nodded again. Carlos removed his hand. "Fuck, and I ran Cameron off."

"We can worry about that later," Cody said exasperated. "Grab some pillows and blankets for the couch for when they bring Nathan, and I'll grab the first aid kit and water."

It didn't take them long to do what was needed. Cody explained Corbin and Nathan. Carlos kept mentally kicking himself for running Cameron off; if he hadn't, they'd be able to get Nathan to a hospital quicker and everyone to safety.

"They're here!" Cody announced, opening the door.

Ryan came in carrying a naked, limp young man followed by Dean and Mitch. Carlos stood there, out of the way, waiting for someone to tell him what to do, if anything. Ryan laid the boy Carlos assumed was Nathan on the couch, propping his head on a pillow. Cody appeared carrying a small bowl of water and a washcloth.

"Clean him up as best you can," Ryan ordered. "Someone get me some water." Dean disappeared into

the kitchenette, returning to hand Ryan the water. He hovered over them worried. "We need to come up with a plan." Ryan cracked the bottle open. He lifted the unconscious boy's head. He pressed the bottle to his lips. "Drink, Nathan."

"Thank God you guys are okay!" Cameron burst through the door, startling everyone.

Mitch snorted angrily, "No thanks to you."

"What? Fuck you. I went to call my Aunt Lexi," Cameron explained. "She said the director checked in with his husband right before he went to visit some dude named Lin."

"Lin Maxwell," Ryan finished.

Cameron finally noticed the naked boy on the couch covered in scabs and blistering bug bites. "Jesus, is he okay?"

The radio Cody brought in crackled to life with Brad's voice. "I called the police. They are sending officers and an ambulance over now. They said it'll be at least an hour before they can get here." There was a collective groan. "I'm sorry guys, the dispatcher said there's some sort of accident that has everyone tied up."

"We can't wait," Ryan pronounced. "Nathan could be dead by then. Lin could be dead by then, if he isn't already." There were murmurs of agreement from the other boys. "Cody, you and Cameron take Nathan to the local hospital. He needs treatment now."

"Got it." Cody looked to Cameron.

Ryan laid Nathan's head back down before standing up and facing them. "The rest of you stay here."

"What are you going to do?" Carlos asked.

Ryan stiffened. "I'm going to the house to see if I can rescue Lin."

"Not without me," Mitch and Dean spoke up almost in unison.

Carlos took a deep breath and contributed, "Or me."

"Wait," Cameron interrupted. "One of you should drive Nathan since you know the way." He tossed the keys to Dean. "Mitch and Ryan can go up the back trail, and Carlos and I can go up the main way."

Carlos gravitated to Cameron. Putting a hand on his shoulder, he asked, "Are you sure?"

Before he could answer, Dean asked angrily, "Why do I have to go?"

"You or Mitch, I don't care," Ryan answered for Cameron. "It's a good plan. You two take the radio and keep Brad up to date, but Carlos comes with me. The other goes with Cameron. We don't want to accidently set off the alert that someone is coming."

"Alert?" Carlos looked at Cameron. He didn't want Cameron going. He wanted Cameron to hop back into his SUV and speed away from all this.

"There's a sensor that goes off when someone goes up the main drive," Cody answered. "Brad and I put it in so Walden knew when someone was coming. All you have to do is cut the wire leading up to the house and you'll be good."

"Wait," Mitch cut in. "Cody, you know the wiring. You go with Cameron. I'll go with Dean."

"But, I don't want to go," Dean complained.

Seeing Ryan was about to lose it, Carlos stepped in. "Enough! Dean and Mitch, get Nathan out of here. Ryan, you're with me. Cody and Cameron, be careful."

That seemed to take the fight out of everyone. "Come on, let's get going."

Carlos saw the gratitude in Ryan's eyes. Dean carefully lifted Nathan from the couch and headed out the door, followed by Mitch. They all stood outside watching Dean begrudgingly start the engine and leave in Cameron's SUV with Nathan and Mitch in the back.

"I'll drive." Cody hopped onto one of the four-wheelers. "I know a short cut."

Carlos put a hand on Cameron's shoulder. "Be careful, Chipmunk."

"You too, Latin Lover." Cameron patted Carlos's hand. They shared a smile.

The rev of an engine broke their moment. Ryan said, "Boys, if you're done, we need to get going."

24

FEAR

CAMERON HELD ONTO Cody tight as they flew through the woods. The newly formed trail was cleared of most of the branches in their way, but the occasional branch still smacked them as they sped. When they pulled out onto the main drive an hour or so later, Cameron was grateful.

They stopped to piss and check in with Brad. He informed them two police cruisers and an ambulance were on the way, but they were still a good forty-five minutes out. He updated them that Mitch and Dean successfully delivered Nathan to an urgent care center and were waiting for news. Then, Cameron and Cody were back on the road.

"Here." Cody stopped the four-wheeler and they got off. "I'll cut the wire and then we can head on up by foot."

"I wish the police would hurry." Cameron looked down the road.

Cody came up beside him. "I know. I'm scared, too."

Cameron didn't correct Cody. He wasn't scared; he was petrified. For them. For Ryan and Carlos. And for the poor unfortunate souls who were trapped up there in that house by two armed men. He couldn't imagine the bravery it took Nathan to escape and make his way to the camp.

"Remember, we don't do anything stupid. We just head up there to see what's going on," Cody reiterated. "If we see a way to rescue everyone, we take it. Otherwise, we head back here and report to Brad."

Cameron wished Carlos and Ryan had taken a radio with them, so Cody would have reiterated the same message to them. There was no way to know if Carlos and Ryan made it through the back trail or not. Ryan said it would only take an hour or so for them, but what if the men were waiting for them?

"Come on," Cameron said with a determination he didn't feel.

They stayed to the edge of the woods, walking quietly up the hundred feet to the house. Cameron's heart thudded in his chest. They could hear men arguing, their voices raised to near shouting. They crept closer. Cameron strained to hear what they were saying.

Cody stopped. Cameron motioned him to continue on, but he shook his head no. He pointed up at the corner of the house. Cameron looked. He saw Carlos. He was crouched down, inching his way forward. Cameron looked for Ryan, but couldn't find him.

What are they doing? Cameron kept scanning for Ryan. He wanted to get Carlos's attention, to let him know that he was there. The only problem was if he did, he risked exposing all of them.

Giving up, Cameron turned his attention back to the two fighting men. Things between them were obviously getting heated. The scrawny, blonde man was frantically pointing back to the house, toward Carlos. The other, a muscular man Cameron recognized but couldn't place, kept slamming his hands into the scrawny man's chest.

Suddenly the muscular man backhanded the other, sending him crashing to the ground. The muscular man pulled out a gun. Cameron watched in horror as the blonde man's body jolted from the impact of each bullet into his frail body. He didn't stop until he heard the click of the metal trigger.

Cameron looked to Carlos, to see what he was doing. "No!" he shouted when Carlos took off running at the man. The man looked down the road to where Cameron was crouched. He took a few steps toward Cameron before Carlos slammed into him.

Seeing Carlos knocked to the ground, Cody raced past Cameron and tackled the man by the waist. Carlos was back up and trying to pin the man's arm down, only to get knocked away again. Cody straddled the man and was punching him in the face, but taking as many blows as he was giving.

Cameron joined the fight, grappling with the man's other arm. He tried to remember some of the things his Aunt Lexi taught him. Something hard came crashing into his body. It was Cody. Cody righted himself and ran back into the man. Cameron saw Carlos struggling to get up on the other side.

Where is Ryan? he wondered.

DON'T DO ANYTHING DUMB OR CAST-IRON SKILLET

CARLOS AND RYAN had made the last leg of their trek by foot. Carlos felt an eerie sense of déjà vu, even though these events weren't quite the same as what happened with Dennis. They were close enough, though, and he wished they had more than their fists and wits to save the day.

"You go that way and sneak around to the front and stay low," Ryan said when they got to the edge of the trail. "I'll go around the other way. There's a barn Walden converted into a playroom. They probably have everyone in there. There's an extra set of keys in the house. If we can get them."

"Nothing foolish," Carlos reminded him. "We go in, see what we can, and then get out."

Ryan huffed. "I wish we brought a radio."

"Me, too." Carlos took Ryan's hand and gave it a squeeze. "Let's do this."

They cautiously pushed their way through the brush. Ryan went left and Carlos went right. Keeping low, he made his way around the house. He could hear two men fighting. He moved closer, crouching at the edge of the house. He could see them: a muscular brunette and a scarecrow of a man. With their voices near shouts, he was just able to hear them.

"That little brat has got to be at the camp!" shouted the brunette.

The scarecrow man shouted back, "There's no way! We would have seen him. I'm telling you he's hiding somewhere around here, Rafi!"

Rafi. Carlos noted the name. The scarecrow man had to be Corbin. Carlos moved a bit closer. He wondered about Ryan's location. He had a sinking feeling Ryan was doing something crazy. *That's why we split up*, Carlos realized too late. He focused back on the two men.

"You know what?! I don't give a fuck anymore." Rafi slammed his hands into Corbin's chest, knocking the man back. "There's no money!"

Corbin steadied himself from the blow. "I swear to you there is money here! We just need to find it."

Rafi pushed Corbin again. "There's no fucking money, you fucking addict."

"Go then!" Corbin shot back. "And don't act like you don't need that fucking money either! How many other men came forward after that fucker in there did? How long was it before you were black-balled by every adult film studio? How long was it before you had to shut down your fan sites because your subscribers got tired of watching you jack off because no one would work with you?"

Rafi pushed Corbin again, nearly knocking the man over. "Don't push me."

"Why do you think I contacted you?" Corbin spat out. "I knew you were desperate for money!"

Rafi knocked Corbin to the ground with a back-handed slap. "I may not be getting my money, but at least I can get my revenge." Carlos held his breath. Rafi pulled a gun from his belt. "And I can shut you the fuck up."

Carlos watched, wide-eyed. Shots rang. Corbin's body jumped with each puncture of hot metal into his body. Rafi didn't stop until he heard the click of an empty magazine. Carlos saw his sinister happy smile. He knew he had to do something now. He only hoped Ryan followed his lead.

Carlos took off running towards the muscular man. He knew he had no hope of taking the man down on his own, but if Ryan jumped in, they might have a chance. Dashing through the cars, Carlos was vaguely aware of hearing Cameron's voice yelling, "No!" and that was the distraction he needed. Rafi was looking down the road when they collided.

Carlos was tossed to the side. He righted himself just in time to see Cody tackle Rafi to the ground where they grappled. Carlos jumped to pin one of his arms to the ground, letting Cody straddle the man's chest so he could rain punches down. Carlos was knocked away again.

Getting up, he saw Cameron wrestling down Rafi's other arm. Before Carlos could get back into the fight,

Rafi used his free hand to knock Cody off of him and into Cameron. Carlos moved to take Cody's place, but took a hit to the face that sent him flying back.

"Fucking bastards!" Rafi spat out, getting up and kicking Cody in the stomach. "You're saving me the trouble of coming next door and slitting your throats while you sleep."

Carlos saw stars in his vision as he struggled to get up. Rafi had his foot raised, ready to stomp on Cameron's head. There was the sound of metal hitting bone and then Rafi's eyes rolled back in his head before he fell over. Carlos, confused for a moment, saw Ryan standing there with a cast-iron skillet in hand.

"I thought we said nothing stupid." Ryan tossed a set of keys to Cody. "Go see if they are in the playroom and bring out some type of restraints."

"Yes, sir," Cody groaned, standing up. Carlos saw Cody's bloody lip and two black eyes.

Once he was standing, Carlos reached down and pulled Cameron up. He saw Cameron's hair was mussed and his face had a few cuts and scrapes, but otherwise he was okay. Carlos wondered how bad he looked, knowing it was probably bad judging by the expression on Cameron's face.

"Hey, tough guy." Ryan squeezed his shoulder. "I thought *I* was the crazy one."

"Leave it to me," Carlos winced. He tasted blood on his lip. "Where did you get the frying pan?"

"Skillet," Ryan corrected. "When I saw they were out front, I broke in the back door to get the keys." Ryan did a practice swing. "I picked this little baby up

when I heard the gunshots. Then I came out here to see you three getting your asses beat."

"Our asses were the only thing he didn't beat." Cameron slinked up beside Ryan. "He did a number on you." He took Carlos's face gently in his hands and moved it side to side. "I don't think you'll be filming anytime soon."

Carlos pulled his face away. "Is that all you're worried about?"

"No," Cameron huffed back at him, taking Carlos in his arms. He mumbled softly into Carlos's ear, "Asshole. Don't you ever do something crazy like that again."

"I promise I will," Carlos said, returning the hug.

"I want to go see Nathan," a naked bald man announced. He was being helped along by another man in his underwear.

"He's in good hands, Lin." Ryan went over and took Lin into his arms. "Mitch and Dean are with him at an urgent care facility. The police should be here within the hour."

"I'm going to give Brad an update," Cody said and started down the path.

"Can we get some clothes?" one of the men in their underwear asked.

Carlos looked at the house then back at the men. "Crime scene."

"Our shit is still in the car." One of the men broke away and headed to the cars. "No offense, Lin, but I'm tired of looking at your twig and berries."

Lin playfully laughed. "Fuck you, Josh."

26

COWARD

CAMERON LAY IN bed with his head resting on Carlos's chest. It was early morning and the sun had yet to rise. He reflected on the past few days and everything that happened. He knew when this story broke, he'd be thrust back into the media limelight, and he still hadn't come clean about his weird connection with Carlos.

He supposed it was because he didn't want the way Carlos looked at him to change. Even with his eyes beginning to swell shut as they waited another thirty minutes for the police to arrive that day, Carlos looked at him with such love. If that look turned to pity, Cameron didn't know what he'd do.

Cameron carefully wrote his name on Carlos's skin with his finger while they waited that day. He made it out of the scuffle with only a split lip and few bruises. Carlos and Cody had not fared as well. Their bodies were littered with bruises which turned deep shades of purple.

Once things settled, Carlos joked with him they could fuck now that the shoot was cancelled. "You're finally going to get your nut, Chipmunk."

Cameron roughly pushed him away, forgetting the bruises and causing Carlos to wince in pain. "I'm so sorry," he cried out, throwing his arms around Carlos and causing him to yelp in pain again.

"Maybe after I've healed," Carlos had grimaced.

He hadn't meant to hurt Carlos then, and he didn't mean to hurt him now. Carefully untangling himself from him, Cameron looked down at the battered, yet handsome and angelic face. He did the one thing Carlos wanted, and he was too stubborn to give, until now. He leaned down and pressed his lips lightly to Carlos's.

Carefully getting out of the bed, Cameron slipped into another set of Carlos's clothes. It was Wednesday and the airlines still hadn't found his luggage, but it didn't matter now. Josh and his crew had packed up all their equipment in the back of Lin's truck and were staying at a local motel in town while the police were doing their investigations.

The police told Carlos and Cameron they were free to go after making their statements, as long as they promised to make themselves available should they be needed. They probably wouldn't be needed since Corbin and Rafi hadn't thought to disable the cameras Lin and Nathan had all over the place for filming.

Sighing, Cameron grabbed his carry-on bag and took one last look at his slumbering Latin lover. Cameron told everyone he was only going to stay until they were able to get the tires fixed on the vehicles,

but that was only an excuse to stay longer than he should. The van's tires were fixed on Monday and Carlos's truck was scheduled to be ready today.

He quietly stepped out of the bedroom and onto the front porch. He looked out over the water to see the first rays of sun peeking up over the trees. For a second, he wished he was sharing this moment with Carlos. He couldn't, though. He'd look into those brown eyes and never want to leave.

"Leaving without saying goodbye?" Cameron jumped at the sound of Ryan's voice to his side. "Coward."

Cameron peered through the dark to see Ryan sitting on their front porch. "What are you doing sitting here in the dark?"

"Contemplating," Ryan answered solemnly. "And making sure you don't leave without saying goodbye to me." Cameron could make out a forced smile on Ryan's face. "The airline called and left a message on the office phone. They found your luggage and wanted to know if you want it shipped here or back to California since you had a return flight booked this morning."

"I, uh, don't know what to say."

Ryan got up and surprised Cameron by giving him a hug. "Say you'll send me back that autographed photo of your aunt."

"I'm going to miss you," Cameron laughed, hugging him back. "Will you say goodbye to all the guys for me?"

Ryan patted Cameron on the back before letting go. "Sure. It'll be good practice."

"Practice?" Cameron questioned.

Ryan let out a deep breath. "Brad and Cody are leaving with Carlos. He's going to help them get settled. Mitch and Dean say they are staying, but I talked to Lin last night at the hospital. He's not sure we should reopen the camp considering why it really took so long for the police to get here."

"There wasn't an accident?" Cameron asked, shocked.

Ryan let out a sound of derision. "Apparently they were thirty minutes from a shift change and none of the officers on duty wanted to come out here and work past their shift. Then the dispatch forgot to pass on the call to the new officers."

"Wow." Ryan was flabbergasted. "How did you find out?"

Cameron saw the impish grin spread across Ryan's face. "One of the officers told me." Ryan winked. "In bed."

"You didn't."

"I did, and I'll tell you all about it over email." Ryan hugged him again. "Go on now before I cry. I don't do tears."

Choked up, Cameron said, "I love you, you big flaming queen."

"I love you too, Chipmunk," Ryan teased. "Now, go. I'll tell everyone goodbye for you."

Cameron moved down to the SUV. Opening the door, he turned back to Ryan. "Tell Carlos …" Cameron debated for a moment on what he wanted Ryan to tell him. "Tell Carlos I kissed him in his sleep." Then he got in the SUV and drove away before Ryan could say anything.

WHAT TO DO

NATHAN STIRRED AWAKE. Daddy Lin was in the chair beside his hospital bed. Nathan's body ached and hurt when he moved, despite the drugs they pumped into him. When he awakened that first time under the bright lights, Daddy Lin was there and hadn't left his side since.

Daddy Lin told him they pulled thirty ticks from his body, but lost count of the thorns and mites. They treated him for dehydration and sent his bloodwork off to see if there was anything else they needed to worry about. His body was slathered with a medical aloe, then wrapped tightly in bandages.

When the nurse left, he pulled the covers off and said to Daddy Lin, "Look. You're a Daddy, and now I'm a Mummy." That made Daddy Lin smile.

"You did good," Daddy Lin told him. "You were brave, and if you hadn't gone to get Ryan, my friends and I would probably be dead now."

Daddy Lin told him everything that happened while he was at the hospital. Corbin being shot. Carlos, Cody, and Cameron trying to take down Rafi. Ryan using the cast iron skillet. Cody setting them free and then waiting around for the police who forgot to come.

"They destroyed the house looking for Daddy Walden's treasure." Nathan saw tears in Daddy Lin's eyes. He let out a soft laugh. "You should have seen Rafi's face when Ryan told him Daddy Walden called *you* his treasure."

Nathan reached out and took Daddy Lin's hand. "Are we going to stay at the camp until the house is fixed?"

Daddy Lin gave his hand a squeeze. "I think we should think about moving someplace closer to civilization. The boys tried to film that porn to attract guests, and we have all been doing fan sites to help keep the power going, but we live too far out to do what's needed to really make money."

"What does Ryan want?" Nathan asked

Daddy Lin sighed. "He wants to try and keep the camp going, and maybe rebrand it."

"Daddy Lin," Nathan said with tremble in his voice, "that place was Daddy Walden's dream. It's where I met Ryan and you."

"I know." Daddy Lin patted his hand. "We'd need a lot of money to get the camp up and running. Even if we did all the work ourselves, it would still cost a pretty penny."

Nathan shifted uncomfortably in the bed. "I don't want to go. What if we did more videos?"

"We'd have to make a ton of videos," Daddy Lin said softly.

Nathan worried Daddy Lin would hate him with what he was about to say. "Can we at least try?" Nathan's eyes watered with guilt. "We can live in the camp with Ryan and the boys so we're not so alone."

"I love you." Daddy Lin stood and hugged Nathan in the bed. "If you want to stay, we will."

Nathan heaved a sigh of relief. "Can we live in the camp from now on?"

"Anything you want, baby. Anything you want."

REALLY? CAN ANYTHING ELSE GO WRONG?

CAMERON GOT OFF the long flight tired and exhausted. His return flight home had two delays and even worse, when he finally landed back home, he had a voicemail from Ryan saying the airline delivered his missing luggage to them and he found the perfect way to get it to him. At this point, Cameron didn't care.

Without any luggage to retrieve, he ordered a ride which never showed. The next ride he ordered turned out to be the circuit queen he fucked in the bathroom. Luckily he didn't recognize Cameron. Five days of no skin routine or product in your hair can do that. Cameron gave him a generous tip and a five star review out of sheer guilt.

He went to unlock the front door, only to remember his keys were in his luggage … which was in Walden Woods. So, he had to ring the bell and hope someone was home. He sat on the front stoop and waited, ringing the bell two more times before calling his Aunt Lexi on his dying phone.

"Oh, honey," she said merrily into the phone, "I'm not home. I'm in Palm Springs on a shoot." Cameron was about ready to cry when the doors swung open and his Aunt Lexi appeared. "Joking! Get your tired ass in here."

"Not funny, Aunt Lexi," Cameron said, struggling to get up.

She looked him up and down. "Neither is this look. We're scheduling you a spa day right away. And, what are you wearing?"

"Can I just take a shower and get something to eat before I rehash this whole horrible trip?" Cameron asked, pausing only to kiss her on the cheek before walking by. "Why are there stairs?!"

A hot shower, some clean clothes, and moisturizer later, Cameron felt more like himself sitting at the kitchen island eating a sandwich. His Aunt Lexi waited until he chewed the last bite before she grilled him. She knew most of it already from their daily phone calls, but Cameron knew she could tell he was holding back. So, he told her about Carlos.

"Awe!" she gushed. "He called you Chipmunk! That raccoon fact is a little disturbing, but awe!"

"He called me Chipmunk because he said I wanted his nut between my cheeks," Cameron explained.

Lexi leaned in. "Did you?"

"Yes," Cameron admitted. "Both sets."

Lexi then asked, "Did you?"

"No," Cameron answered with disappointment.

"Why not?"

Cameron just stared at her for a moment. "He had the shoot to do, and then there was this weird hostage situation where we got our asses beat."

Lexi made a face. "Oh, yeah, that. Anyway, did you at least exchange information?"

"No. He lives on the East coast and he's friends with Dennis and Billy. It would be strange." Cameron narrowed his eyes at his Aunt Lexi. She was thinking. "Whatever it is you're planning, don't."

"Whatever do you mean?" she feigned mock indignation. "I was just thinking about that Ryan guy, the one that calls me Sexy Lexi. I want to meet him. He sounds fun."

Cameron got up from the stool. "I'm going to take a nap. I want to put all this behind me before it blows up all over social media again."

"Of course." Cameron didn't like the smile she wore. "I'll wake you for dinner." Cameron put his dishes in the dishwasher while she typed away at her screen, then put the phone to her ear. The last thing he heard her say was, "Hello? Is this Ryan? Fabulous. I hear you're my biggest fan. This is Sexy Lexi Luscious."

QUESTIONS, ANSWERS, AND A PHONE CALL

I T BOTHERED CARLOS that Cameron left without even saying goodbye. Ryan told him what he said, about kissing him in his sleep. He didn't believe it. Cameron had been so adamant about not kissing he knew it was just something he told Ryan to tell him to make him feel good.

When they had got home, the house was empty and he was able to get Brad and Cody settled in the pool house. While unpacking, he found a suitcase which didn't belong to him. Cody and Brad didn't recognized it either. When they opened it, they found a note from Ryan.

*Guess you'll have to find your Chipmunk
to give him back his things, Latin Lover*

*Love,
Ryan*

Carlos set the suitcase in the corner of his room, not knowing what to do. He had no way of finding Cameron and didn't know why Ryan thought he would. When he called Walden Woods to ask Ryan, he got the machine. Ryan called him back thirty minutes later.

"My dear," Ryan said into the phone with wickedness in his voice, "if you don't know how to find him, I can't help you. I'm surprised you didn't recognize him. Now, I made a promise not to tell, but maybe one of your mutual friends can help. Give Brad and Cody my love. Talk to you later!"

Ryan had hung up before he could question him any further. That was when he heard Hunter downstairs.

"Carlos!" Hunter bellowed. "What did you do to the tires on my truck?!"

He figured it was time to break the news. He got out of bed, his body still sore from the fight and long drive. He looked in the mirror to see the bruises on his face hadn't faded. In fact, they looked worse. He readied himself for the barrage of questions to which he had no answer.

Hunter's anger faded when he saw Carlos's face. Of course Mark, Dennis, and Benjamin were there as well. He was assaulted with questions and only when he had assured them all he was okay, did they sit down

for Carlos to relive the entire ordeal again. When he was done, everyone sat staring at Carlos in disbelief.

Mark was the first to speak. "Okay, what are we now? Some gay porn crime-solving gang? All I know is nothing like this had better happen during Hunter's and my wedding."

Everyone turned to look at Mark. Hunter had his hand in his head and said, "This isn't how I wanted to tell everyone, Mark."

With everyone's attention on Hunter and Mark, no one noticed when Carlos answered the call from Billy. "Hey! Chipmunk!"

"Chipmunk? Why are you calling me chipmunk?" Carlos questioned.

"Billy! He's Latin Lover!" Carlos heard Jordan, Billy's boyfriend, shout at him.

There was a pause as Billy thought about it. "I guess that makes sense, but he could be a Latin chipmunk."

"Billy, I don't have time for your deep thoughts," Carlos groaned into the phone. "I've been through Hell and back."

"I heard," Billy said conspiratorially. "Since you're not going to be working for a while, I thought it would be a good idea if you came out for a visit."

Carlos sighed. "Billy, I'm in no … wait. How do you know I'm not going to be working for a while?"

"Same way I know you should bring that suitcase," Billy answered cryptically.

"Billy."

"Chipmunk lover!" Billy paused. "Wait, that's not right."

Carlos heard Jordan correcting him again. "Latin Lover! You know what! Give me that phone."

"No! Call him on your own phone!" Billy yelled back.

Jordan threatened, "Give me the phone, or I won't let you touch my butt!"

"I'll do it anyway!" Billy countered.

Carlos put his phone on speakerphone, then put his head in his hand. The other men in the room stopped talking and listened to Billy and Jordan fighting over the phone. They all stifled their laughter at the bizarre and sexual threats they tossed at each other.

Ten minutes later, Jordan won with the threat of showing everyone the video of Billy singing karaoke. "Carlos? Are you still there?"

Carlos looked up from his hand and saw everyone was staring at him. "Yes."

"There's a ticket with your name on it for whenever you want to use it." Jordan took a moment to catch his breath. "Use it soon. There's a chipmunk here that could use your nut."

"Jordan! You weren't supposed to say anything," Carlos heard Billy shout. Then more wrestling, then groans. Carlos hung up before he could hear anymore.

Carlos couldn't believe it. Billy and Jordan knew Cameron. That's what Ryan meant when he said they were intertwined. That's why he put the suitcase in the back of the truck. More importantly, Cameron wanted to see him.

"You said this chipmunk's name is Cameron?" Dennis asked, scrolling through his phone. "Not Cameron Matthews, by any chance?"

Carlos thought for a moment. "Yeah, I think so. Why?"

Dennis motioned for them all to watch the television as he cast Cameron's very public break up with Alex.

EPILOGUE

CAMERON LAY BY the pool in his blue bikini swim briefs. Just as he suspected, someone had gotten hold of the kidnapping story and he went viral all over again. Instead of dealing with the public, he decided to lay low at the house and miss Carlos. He knew he could ask his Aunt Lexi to have Billy contact Carlos, but it was better this way. A clean break.

The upside of the whole situation was Walden Woods was now on the gay radar. Ryan emailed him saying since the story broke, they were turning down reservations. Aunt Lexi fronted the money for the renovations, and they were in full gear. They planned on having internet by Christmas. Ryan also described in great detail how his cop frisked him and gave him cavity searches.

Another upside was they forgot about all the footage on the cameras before Josh took them. He liked what he saw and asked his Aunt Lexi if he was available for more shoots as a director's assistant. They released what was shot while the story of the camp was still hot, and they listed Cameron as the director.

Overall, everything turned out well. Sure, he was once again a media prisoner in his aunt's home, and every time his name was mentioned the breakup video with Alex showed up. Then, there were the speculations about Carlos and him. Those hurt most because they weren't an item and probably would never be.

"Cameron!" His Aunt Lexi called from the house. "Your luggage is here!"

Cameron took a long sip of his mango smoothie, then leaned back in the chair and closed his eyes. He shouted back, "Put it in my room, please!"

"Cameron!" His Aunt Lexi called again. "You have a special delivery!"

Cameron groaned. "Put it in my room! I'll open it later!" Cameron settled down in the lounge chair, letting the sun beat down on him. He felt a shadow creep over him. He blinked open his eyes. He couldn't believe what he was seeing. "Carlos?

"Hey, Chipmunk." Carlos gave him a cocky grin. "This special delivery wants you to open his package now."

Cameron got up and hugged Carlos tight before remembering his bruising. "Oh, I'm so sorry. Did I hurt you?"

"Only when you didn't say goodbye." Carlos wrapped his arms around Cameron tight.

Cameron grinned. "I'm sorry about that, how can I make it up to you?"

"I have some free time while I'm checking out film schools." Carlos grinned brightly. "How about a date or two? Maybe show me around the area?"

Cameron pulled back slightly. "You're not moving out here just to be with me are you?"

"Conceited much?" Carlos pulled him back close. "That's an added bonus. I'm going to be staying in Billy's empty apartment if I decide to go to school out here."

Cameron asked coyly, "Would a kiss get you to move out here?"

"Hhmm ..." Carlos pretended to think. "A kiss is so *intimate*. You do owe me a fuck, though."

Both of them laughed when they heard Aunt Lexi yell, "Get that nut, Chipmunk!"

"I've always wanted to kiss a Latin Lover." Cameron leaned in.

"I don't kiss." Carlos turned his head to block Cameron's lips. "Too intimate."

"Not more intimate than having your tongue in my–"

And Carlos cut Cameron off with a kiss.

1. The story opens with Cameron hooking up with a stranger. Is this dangerous behavior or part of his healing process?

2. Carlos notices how sensual the sex is with Mask and Mark, do you think this changes Carlos's view of sex?

3. Nathan and Lin Maxwell (Daddy Lin) is a nontraditional relationship with nontraditional power dynamics. Do you think this type of relationship can work in the real world?

4. Lin is the face of Walden Woods, while Ryan and Nathan are the owners. Ryan explains this is because Lin is "masc" while Ryan is "fem" and people would rather rent from Lin. Is this a true concept?

5. Why do you think Brad and Cody did not take the obvious next step in their relationship?

6. Cameron says he doesn't kiss because it's too intimate. Considering what he does sexually, do you agree? Why or why not?

7. Ryan is basically the only person not in a relationship at the camp. Do you think this affects him?

8. When Carlos leaves, Brad and Cody leave with him. Why do you think they did this?

9. Cameron stayed with his fiancé, even after he caught him cheating. Do you think if the announcement of him cheating again wasn't so public, Cameron would still be with him?

10. Cameron is a little put-off when he thinks Carlos is moving across the country to just be with him. Is this a proper response?

ROBBY LEWIS IS a Gay Erotica writer based out of Charleston, South Carolina. When he's not busy tending his plants, being a doggy daddy, or watching the latest Sci-Fi, he can be found creating Gay Erotica for his readers that challenge conventional sexual roles. He's influenced by writers such as T.J. Klune, Rhys Ford, Jordan Castillo Price, and L.A. Witt. You can keep up with Robby Lewis's latest releases and antics on his social media at Dreams – Robert J. Lewis (robert-j-lewis.com).